*Book Six*

# Kings and Crusaders

## Chapter One

We got the word in Cornwall when Simon's galley came in from London with a cargo of archer recruits and bales of Egyptian linen for our tailors to make into tunics for them. King Richard is dead of being a fool—he got too close to a castle wall he and his men were attacking for no good reason and a boy got him with a crossbow.

Richard's brother John is to replace him and my priestly brother Thomas and I are trying to decide whether or not to go to London for

John's crowning to be our new king. We are thinking about taking my son George and half a dozen or so of the older boys in Thomas's school with him—and two galleys full of our steadiest archers in case there is a problem or misunderstanding in London.

As you might imagine, we have had quite a debate about whether or not we should attend. Thomas thinks we should go and I am not so sure.

"London is too big to ignore any longer. We already need our own agent and some kind of post in London—and if we continue to prosper, George and the boys will certainly need an agent there to represent them when they take over the company of archers. We will have to go to London sooner or later to begin making arrangements for an agent to represent us and find a safe place where he can live and our coins will be safe—so we might as well go sooner and kill two or three ducks with one stone."

I just looked at my priestly brother without saying a word. So he ploughed on without stopping as he always does when he has made up his mind.

"If we go now, George and the boys can see both the King getting his crown and the size of London and how people live there. Then you can bring George and the boys back to Cornwall, and I can go on to Rome with the Pope's share of the contributions we took off last year's refugees and pilgrims for the Pope's prayers."

I was still not so sure it was a good idea, and I said as much.

"I am not so sure it is wise to go and be seen. It will remind John and what is his name, the Pope's arrogant new nuncio, of our existence and that we are not paying much in way of tithes and taxes."

*We were paying none at all, as a matter of fact—because Cornwall is so poor that even the Romans did not build a road to it. That was what we always said when anyone asked for taxes and donations. It has been working, at least so far— and spit over your shoulder and knock on wood that it continues.*

Thomas disagreed. "Nonsense, you are going to be in England all the rest of the summer and neither of us needs to be here in Cornwall for the next couple of weeks to oversee the training of the apprentice archers. The same applies to the construction work on the new curtain walls going up at Restormel and Launceston. Besides, Henry is here; he can look after the men's training and make sure the construction continues."

***** *William*

Thomas does have a point. I was in Cornwall for the summer because several years ago I came to my senses and began spending winters on Cyprus and in the Holy Land and summers in England instead of the other way around as I did during our first few years in Cornwall.

Thomas and the rest of my family, on the other hand, are always here at Restormel—except for Thomas's annual trip to Rome to pay the Pope his share of the coins the refugees and pilgrims contribute for the Pope's prayers for their safety whilst they are on our galleys.

*It is amazing how many of our passengers throw in coins when our galley sergeants pass the bucket for the Pope's prayers; it is also amazing how few of those coins reach the Pope. Oh well, it works, and everyone who makes it safely is satisfied—and those who do not survive their voyages are either dead or Moorish slaves and cannot complain.*

There is good reason for us to want Cornwall to be forgotten. We do not want the King to even think about Cornwall when he tries to raise money for his wars. John, the damn fool, is already rumoured to be thinking about another campaign in France even though most of his barons are said to be opposed to the idea—it is said the barons are opposed to another war by the King because they know their taxes and scutages will be increased to pay for it.

The barons are also afraid the King will take them off to war and their neighbours who pay the King's scutage fee to buy out of serving in the campaign will try to take over some of their lands and women and serfs whilst they are gone.

What the barons are really most afraid of, of course, is that they will get themselves killed or die of the poxes that seem to afflict soldiers when they do not wear the proper garlic cloves and say the proper prayers. That is exactly what happened to dear old Edmund those many years ago and resulted in us coming to Cornwall and settling here.

Thomas thinks we will have nothing to fear from our new king because Cornwall is so inconsequential to him—because it is so poor and its revenues so small. According to Thomas, the King knows Cornwall can barely support one or two knightly fiefs, so why would he even bother with us?

Moreover, as Thomas pointed out to me with a great deal of satisfaction in his voice after he took a sip of his morning bowl of ale, we are in the new king's good book—we were not allied with the nobles who supported Richard against John when John tried to stay on the throne. To the contrary, we bought the earldom and Cornwall's nine small manors from John himself when he was regent and Richard still king.

"We will," Thomas concluded with a great deal of satisfaction after a big gulp of ale and a little belch, "be safe if we go to London for the coronation. No one around the King gives a damn about Cornwall."

It is true. Cornwall does have tin mines, but they belong to the King so he already gets all of their very substantial revenues. It also has some monasteries and church lands which are not valuable to anyone because their revenues, such as they are, all go to the Church.

Other than tin and the nine manors, Cornwall is mostly fishermen and quite poor—so poor even the Romans did not bother to build a road to it. The road the Romans built to Exeter is a two-day walk from where Cornwall begins at the River Tamar and connected to it by only a rough cart path.

\*\*\*\*\*

After much discussion, I gave in to my brother. Thomas and I will go to London for John's crowning and George and the older boys in Thomas's school will go with us. We are mostly going because Thomas thinks it is time for George and the older boys to see London. He wants them to see what it is like to live in a city so huge it has three castles and almost twenty-five thousand people living in it. Doing for George is the argument that tips the balance.

*My priestly brother is probably right. He usually is what with having read the Bible and all nine books at the monastery before he rescued me from being a serf in our village when our mum died. He is the one who taught me to scribe and jabber in Latin and do sums. It helped pass the time in camp and did not seem to weaken me at all as some of the men warned it might.*

Helen does not want to go because of our infant daughter. She will stay in Cornwall with Ann and our two little ones. Ann being the sister Helen's mother sent to me from Beirut and Helen sent to my bed when she was pregnant with my daughter. They are wonderful wives and dear to me.

Now, of course, they are both pregnant again—and they are both talking about how much I would enjoy being in Cyprus this coming winter with their youngest sister to look after me so they can stay in Cornwall and care for their children.

# Chapter Two

*Sailing for London.*

We were a formidable force as we pushed off from the floating wharf on the River Tamar and set out for London in two fully crewed galleys—Jeffrey's and Harold's. Everyone except the handful of sailors on each galley was a fully trained archer armed with a longbow and one of the new long-handled pikes with a blade and hooks, the ones Brian and his smiths are making for us at our post on Cyprus. And, of course, each of the galleys has its usual complement of one hundred and sixty swords and galley shields for the men to carry when they are ashore.

Our force was particularly large both because we have my son George to guard and because after London we would be splitting up.

I will return to Cornwall on Harold's galley with George and the boys whilst Thomas and a galley full of archers sail to Rome to hand the Pope some of the coins we have collected from our passengers for his prayers. *It is important to keep the Pope sweet. That way, if necessary, we can claim to be acting in his name when we deal with foreign lords and port officials about carrying pilgrims and refugees.*

Peter and Raymond are sailing with us— Peter with me in Jeffrey's galley; Raymond with Thomas and the boys in Harold's. They will stay in London for a while to buy more brood mares and then lead some of the archers on to Derbyshire to collect this year's horses and recruits.  Peter and Raymond and their men will then continue on overland with our horses through Devon and all the way to Cornwall.

Thomas and the six boys are on Harold's galley and will be sleeping in hammocks in the bigger deck castle in the stern where the galley's sailors usually sleep.  Ranulph, the assistant master of Thomas's school, will put the learning on the younger boys whilst Thomas is off to London and Rome.  Ranulph is the scribe Thomas found in Rome to replace Angelo Priestly when he and two of Thomas's boys caught the sweating pox and died two summers ago.

Harold's sailors are undoubtedly not happy about giving up their deck castle to Thomas and the boys.  But they are used to sleeping rough and they will survive—they have already taken an old leather sail and used it to make a comfy shelter for themselves back by where the rudder men steer the galley.

I myself am traveling to London on Jeffrey's galley with Peter Sergeant. We three are sharing the captain's little castle on the deck at the front of the galley. Each of our galleys has about one hundred and thirty men on board—ten to twelve sailors and one hundred and twenty or so of our best archers. The archers sleep huddled together on and around their rowing benches with their legs pulled up under their long and hooded sheepskin coats.

Peter has proven to be invaluable and is now one of my lieutenants with six black stripes on the front and back of his archer's tunic. When Thomas puts aside his bishop's robes and wears his archer's tunic, he also has six stripes of a lieutenant as do Henry, Harold, and Yoram who commands our all-important post and galley hub in Cyprus.

Our most senior sergeants, which includes Raymond and all the survivors of our original company of archers, have five stripes; galley and our cog captains and their equivalents four; regular sergeants three; chosen men two; fully trained archers one; and apprentice archers and everyone else none.

\*\*\*\*\*

The amount of coins Thomas will carry to the Pope is always small because no one except me and Thomas and Yoram in Cyprus knows how many "coins for the Pope's prayers" the refugees and pilgrims donate for the Pope's prayers for their safety—but it is an effective payment for the Pope's personal protection because we put the coins directly into the Pope's hands without any of them being skimmed off by the Italian churchmen who surround him and actually run the Church. They are all thieves down there, are not they?

Soliciting prayer coins from our passengers for the Pope's prayers for their safety at sea was Yoram's idea. It is a splendid coin maker for us in addition to buying the Pope's goodwill and protection.

*As described in an earlier parchment, the archers collect donations from the pilgrims and other passengers they carry and send them directly to the Pope for his prayers for their safety whilst traveling on the sea. Thomas drafted the decree establishing the Order of Poor Landless Sailors and paid the Pope to sign it and name him Bishop of Cornwall as his personal*

*representative to collect and deliver the Pope's*
*share of the takings.*

The real purpose of our collecting money for the Pope's prayers, of course, is to buy some measure of the Pope's protection from the King and the Church and their officials whilst we are carrying out our long-run objective of obtaining more wealth from the world beyond England—whilst appearing in England to be a good but very poor family of Norman origin with a powerful protector.

Thomas and I do not actually know if we have Norman blood, of course, and probably do not since we were birthed as serfs; so we act like everyone else and claim we do. Who would know? We will explain it to George when he gets a little older.

The other provisions of the Pope's decree establishing the Order of Poor Landless Sailors are absolutely splendid so far as we are concerned. They should be since Thomas himself scribed the decree and delivered the initial pouch of coins needed to get the Pope to sign the decree without reading it too closely.

The Pope probably made his mark on it because he and the Italians around him had never even heard of Cornwall or, if they did, considered it so small and meaningless it could be safely ignored—which certainly would be the case if it was not the home base of our archers.

Among the decree's key provisions is the naming of the Earls of Cornwall as the Order's grand masters in perpetuity. Equally important, at least from my perspective because the Church is constantly interfering in earthly matters to increase its wealth and its powers, the decree grants the Order, and thus me as Cornwall's Earl and my heirs, the right to reject any bishops, monks, and priests we do not want in Cornwall.

It also grants the Earls of Cornwall the right to legitimise all of our children to insure the continuation of our line and the Order the Earl commands—and, thus, of course, the continuation of the little linen sack of gold coins my heirs and our agents will directly place into the Pope's hands each year in the years to come when Thomas is no longer available to deliver them.

*Monk's note: William's young wife and her sisters and their children were obviously the cause of the provision legitimising all of his children. Indeed, it seems William and Thomas were already searching for sisters for George in order to keep him away from the tavern girls and their poxes. It is probably also safe to say the Pope would never have signed the decree creating the Order if he had known what the archers would do with the various powers and recognitions he and the King granted them in return for their coins.*

## Chapter Three
*Thomas in London*

"Oars in. Standby with the mooring lines," Harold shouted from the deck at the very front of the galley.

George and the boys were standing wide-eyed next to me on the roof of the stern castle of

Harold's galley as we approached the quay where our galleys and cogs usually moor when they are in London. The boys have been standing up here with me for several hours as we followed Harold's galley up the Thames as it threaded its way through and past the mass of cogs and other cargo transports at anchor in London's harbour and moored at its various wharves and quays.

From the looks on the boys' faces and their words it seems they are surprised and awed by what they see—they have never before seen such a big city or so many boats and people.

"Look," George suddenly shouted. "There is Father and Lieutenant Peter."

And so it was. Harold's galley was immediately in front of us and I could see my brother and Peter climbing up from the deck to get on the quay. A few moments later they saw us and waved and start walking to us.

*Of course George travels separately from his father whenever possible—if either galley went down, we would still have the other and our family and plans could continue.*

"Hello, young man; hello, brother," William said as he reached down to grab George's extended arm and pulled him up on to the quay—and gave him a big hug. Then he and Peter began reaching down and pulling the other boys up. The tide was out and it was some distance from our galleys deck up to the quay— so Harold and Raymond and I lifted them up one at a time to stand on the deck railing and steadied them from behind until they could be pulled the rest of the way up to the quay.

When all six of the boys were safely up on the stone quay, I climbed on to the galley's railing myself and William and Peter hauled me up whilst Harold and Raymond pushed on my arse to help me on my way.

Both William and Peter are carrying swords and wearing chain mail under their tunics. I am too—under my bishop's robe—and so are Harold and Raymond. The archers who scrambled up on to the quay with us to act as our guards are all carrying longbows and small, rounded galley shields in addition to the swords archers are sometimes issued when they go ashore or are trying to board at potential prize.

*We are not taking any chances and none of our men are carrying our new long-handled bladed pikes because we do not want anyone to know we have them.*

"Everything all right?" William silently mouthed to me with a questioning look as I came up from the galley's deck and he gave me a big hug and a pat on the back.

"Aye, it is," I mouthed back with a nod, and then loudly added a comment so all can hear. "Well, lads, here we are in London all safe and sound; God be praised."

"A fish jumped out of the water this morning and landed on our deck. I touched it, I did. One of the archers threw it back in," one of the boys excitedly told William.

"Did he, now, Tom? Well, that was certainly a strong fish to jump so far, was not it?"

"How did it go?" I mouthed to William. "Any problems?"

William shook his head and said, "I am surprised we could not find mooring space closer to Freddy's stables. We will move closer when a better berth opens up. In the meantime, we will have to walk.

"Come on, lads, we are going to have to walk a ways to visit with an old friend. He has got a lot of horses; yes, he does."

Harold turned to William and said, "Send a messenger if you need more men or think of anything. I will be moving both galleys further down the quay as soon as better spaces open up."

Harold said it as William and I started to walk in one direction with the boys towards the stable, and Harold headed off in the other direction with Jeffrey to arrange for water and supplies. Peter and Raymond came with us and so did a guard of more than a dozen heavily armed archers.

After a pause, whilst he stepped around a worker taking a shite on the quay, Harold must have thought of something for he yelled an explanation over his shoulder as to why he was not walking with us.

"Me and Jeffrey will be at the chandler's buying chickens and sheep and such for us to eat whilst we are here and on our outward sailings. Jeffrey needs to take on more food and firewood if his men are to have enough to get all the way to Lisbon without stopping."

Thomas could not contain himself after listening to Harold. He waved his hands about and spoke to the boys.

"What Lieutenant Harold just told the Captain makes good sense and is something for you boys to remember when you are sergeants. He is thinking ahead; yes, he is; he is making sure the men on both galleys will have enough food to eat and water to drink.

"It is good he is doing so. You and the men will need food and water when you sail back to Cornwall on Harold's galley with your father—and Jeffrey and his men will need it if we are to get all the way to Lisbon as the first stop on the even longer voyage I am going to make to Rome on Jeffrey's galley. Food and water go fast when the men are rowing—and there is not much room on a galley's deck for chickens and firewood and sheep and such no matter how much you cripple them up and cram them in.

"The need for galleys and cogs to periodically take on more water and supplies is why the galley Sergeant Jeffrey and I will be on will have to make two or three port calls along the way before we get to Rome. You will need to keep such things in mind when you are the ones who are sending galleys and cogs off on long voyages."

****** *Thomas*

Harold and Jeffrey had moored our galleys at a busy quay. Almost all of the mooring spaces along its entire length were filled with cogs of various sizes, and there is activity all along it with pony carts and carrier men carrying things on and off the cogs and talking and shouting everywhere. Some of the men who see us walking past were openly curious. They stared at us as we passed by and a few of them nodded and smiled at the boys. *It is little wonder they are curious—a bishop, a handful of boys, and several dozen heavily armed men walking together is not an everyday occurrence on the quay.*

After a bit of walking over the quay's rough stones, we came to a big and battered old cog with a great crowd of men standing on the quay next to it. They were merchants from the look of them and the way they are watching each other intently and whispering into each other's ears when they talked.

I was carrying a rolled up parchment map under my arm and saw the big cog and the merchants as yet another opportunity to put learning on the boys.

"Look there, boys," I said. "The big, two-masted cog there with all the sails looks as if it just came in from some distant place where the people do not speak proper English and may not even be Christians. And all those men gathered in front of it are probably merchants who want to buy her cargo."

"Where's she from and what is she carrying?" I asked one of the men as we walked past. The man was not as well-dressed as the merchants but better dressed than many of the workers and hostlers on the quay—probably one of the merchants' clerks.

"She is in from the Finns with ploughs and leather and suchlike."

Without further ado, I hiked up my bishop's robe and knelt down on the quay and spread out the parchment I had been carrying under my arm. It was a map.

The archers hung back whilst the others gathered around me. The men on the quay, and particularly the merchants, were openly curious. A few of them even moved a couple of steps towards us to see what I was doing and try to listen.

*A man wearing a bishop's robe and mitre kneeling on a quay to study a parchment map with a half dozen boys and a couple of dozen heavily armed men gathering around him is not a common occurrence on the London quays and wharves. It is sure to be talked about all day on the quay and nearby wharves and discussed in various local taverns and alehouses this evening.*

"Come from the Finns, eh? Well, that is interesting; yes, it is.

"Tom, show me where you think this cog came from. Point it out. You too, Mark. Ah, right you are. Good on you, Tom; good on you."

\*\*\*\*\*

The stalls in Freddy's huge stable were mostly empty and terribly foul and full of horse shite as usual. It is obviously been a number of days since they had been mucked out to drain off into the harbour. Freddy's is a large stable and there were a number of horses and hostlers about as we walked in. Raymond and I had been here several times previously but William and Peter and everyone else had not. We could hear a smith swearing as he and one of the hostlers tried to get a shoe on a reluctant mare.

"Hold her, damn it, hold her."

And there is the man we are looking for— a tall, cavernous man with a greedy look on his lopsided face; and greedy and conniving is how he should look being as how he trades in horses and runs a stable.

*I would wager he got kicked by a horse, a very big horse from the looks of his face. If I think of it, I will ask the alewife at the White Horse what happened; alewives know everything.*

"Ah, Freddy. There you are," I said.

"Hoy, Youz Eminenz. Youz is welcome here for zure, Bizhop, that youz iz; and hoy to youz too, Raymond. Iz it horzez and cartz youz be needin?"

"Perhaps, Freddy, perhaps; but not until Sunday coming," I answered.

"Today, we are looking for a reasonable place near the quay where we can station someone regular-like to be our agent with the merchants and such. On Sunday afternoon next, however, when Prince John finally gets his crown, we will need three wains and hostlers who know the way to take us up to Saint Peter's

Abbey in Westminster. We will be going up to Westminster so these fine young lads here can watch our new king get his crown."

*We would walk up to Westminster and back if it was just me and William and the men. But Westminster was so far, the boys might get tired—and I did not want our guards to be tired if trouble started.*

"Do not youz fretz about a playz for youz man. Oov got me a right good friend who dealz in houzez an zhopz an zuch, hazen't I?"

"Well, that is good to know, Freddy; yes, it is. If your friend knows of any shops or houses available near the quay, he can find us at the White Horse or on the quay. We are down at the far end with two galleys. Mind you, it cannot be too many coins; we are not rich, are we?" I said.

Then I continued.

"We will probably be sleeping on our galleys if we cannot find a proper inn, would not we? I expect we will have to do that as I have got these boys with me as you can see. They are likely lads; they have come with me to see John get his crown and have a look at London.

"Good lads they are; pass the word for your hostlers and smiths to keep an eye out for them and help them if it seems they need it. We will take handsome care of anyone who helps them if they need it."

*What I do not do is introduce William as my brother. There is no need for anyone to know who William is or that he is even in London, is there?*

"Eminenz; zum Templarz menz waz here two dayz ago. Asking, they waz, about youz.

Haz zem tunics with a big red crozz, do not theyz?"

"Were they, now? Templars you say. Did they leave a message?"

"No. Not a word. But theyz got a big moneztery near the tower, do not theyz? Probablyz thaz where they will be."

"Well, please tell them where to find us if they come again. The Templars are good men, do not you know. Good friends of ours for certain." *They are really not friends at all, but there is no sense saying it and pissing them off when they hear about it.*

"Oh. By the by, Freddy, can you find us some more young brood mares and fillies with good bottoms? About the same number as last year would do for us if you can find them."

Then I explained the situation to Freddy whilst Peter and Raymond listened intently and nodded their heads in agreement. Raymond's agreement is important. He knows horses and sergeants, all of ours, and the men who ride them. *Peter is like me and William and barely knows one end of a horse from the other. He is nodding his head to support Raymond.*

"Some of the men with us will be going on to Derbyshire to get this year's brood mares and young fillies from Hathersage and recruit apprentice archers along the way. Strong amblers for our messengers to ride long distances is what we want the mares to produce. If the coins and horses are right, we would be interested in buying as many as a dozen mares and fillies for breeding stock. Maybe even more if the prices and horses are particularly good."

*Peter and Raymond will be taking the
horses overland to Cornwall as we have done for
the past three summers and, hopefully, will be
doing in the years ahead until our herd is large
enough—having strong horses and archers
trained to ride them is part of our plan for
George and his future. Taking them to Cornwall
overland is not a problem these days; not even
the Earl of Devon is stupid enough try to stop us
or steal them, not with one of our archers leading
or riding every horse, he would not—not unless
he has a death wish.*

"Ooz will getz zum good onez for youz,
would not I?  Howz zoon iz you wantz zem?"

"Any time before or after John gets his
crown will do.  Our men are already here but
there is no hurry—we will wait a week or two or

even more for the right horses, but only if they are good value for our coins.

"We have brought our own hostlers and smiths, but if the coins are right, we would also think seriously about buying a couple of good wains for the mares to pull.  If we do, the wains we will be wanting will be good two-horse wains for carrying our tents and grain for the horses and such, not two-wheel carts, mind you."

# Chapter Four

*King John finally gets a crown.*

John looked splendid at his crowning and so did almost everyone else in attendance. I was wearing my mitre and carrying my crozier, but everyone else in our party looked so poor in their plain Egyptian tunics it is a wonder they were allowed to enter. But they did—they got in without even having to bribe the guards at the church door because our fortune was good.

We all got in without having to pay a bribe because we arrived at Saint Peter's early, and I took the boys for a last-minute piss and shite in the alley behind the abbey—the alley that runs in front of the little door the priests use when they need to relieve themselves or walk to the abbey where they have their rooms and take their meals.

In the alley I saw Hubert Walter, the new Archbishop of Canterbury, and kissed his ring after he finished pissing against the abbey wall and shook his dingle. Hubert is one of Richard's many long-time followers who quickly changed sides and joined John as soon as Richard got himself killed.

Hubert and I are friends, being fellow bishops and all. We have gotten on famously ever since we met two summers ago. That was when Raymond and I and some of Raymond's riders stopped for a bowl of ale in Luton whilst on our way to Derbyshire to get our annual rent of brood mares and recruits.

Hubert had seen me come in the alehouse with my men and introduced himself as a fellow bishop. During our conversation, he found out I had been on the Third Crusade with Richard and used the tavern owners in Sarum to gull old Kerfuffle and his men out of their weapons and horses.

Hubert had been awaiting his appointment as the Bishop of Salisbury when we gulled Kerfuffle out of his arms and gulled his men into getting drunk and breaking into houses to get the city's women. He had been in Sarum soon thereafter and had heard all about what happened, but he had not known why.

Kerfuffle and his men were long gone by then, of course, so Hubert had not gotten the whole story until I told him. He had roared with laughter and stood me a bowl when I finished telling him what we had done and why.

What I did not tell Hubert at the time, and he still does not know, is why William and I and the archers left Richard's service and made our marks on a contract with Lord Edmund. We left because of how Richard treated the three thousand Saracens who surrendered to us at Acre. Richard got them to give up the fortress when he gave his oath he had let them go home to Saladin if they gave up their weapons and surrendered—and then most foully murdered all three thousand of them when they did.

It was stupid to kill the Saracens who surrendered, in addition to being foul—for it got the heathens all riled up when Richard murdered their men after giving his word they would be released. It upset them so much that recruits flooded into Saladin's army and many a good crusader ended up getting himself killed. What made it worse was that Richard suddenly decided to end his crusade and left us out there to face the revenge-seeking Saracens without a commander. *Not a man of his word was our Richard. I do not know much about John but he could not be worse, could he?*

I gestured at William and the boys who were standing in a line with their tunics hiked up and pissing against the abbey wall.

"That is William of Cornwall and his heir and his . . . er . . . pages. They have come all this way to show their support and respect for the new king. Can you help me get them in?"

William was not decked out in the colourful and furry finery worn by Richard's other lords—who seem to be competing to outdo each other in the elegance of their clothes. All William was wearing was a plain, tan Egyptian tunic with the seven stripes of the archers' captain on the front and back and a little cross over his heart to show he had been on a crusade.

At my suggestion, William was wearing his archer's tunic over his chain mail shirt and we both had our wrist knives strapped on under our tunics where they could not be seen. *I do not believe in taking chances; every man here would kill us if he thought he had gain from it.*

"Not there, young Albert," I said. "If you must shite, go over there away from the church wall . . . and be careful where you step." *It has not rained since before we got here and the shite from the priests is really piling up. The rats and birds cannot keep up with the priests unless it rains, can they?*

***** *William*

Thomas motioned for us to hurriedly follow him, so we all dutifully followed him and the regally attired bishop he had been talking to as they pissed side by side against the wall. The fancy bishop raised his crozier to get our attention and then motioned for us to follow as he led us into the church through the priest's door. Then he quickly disappeared into the assembling crowd, and Thomas led us off to the side of the altar where there was more room to stand.

John's coronation was quite a sight even though the stench in the crowded room became increasingly unbearable as more and more people jammed into the church. Everything could be seen because the shutters had been removed from the church's windows so the sun could shine in. Unfortunately, there was no breeze to bring in fresh air as well.

And, of course, being as the coronation was being held in a church and was so important, there were a fortune's worth of candles burning to impress everyone and heat the church even more. Fortunately, we were close enough so we could see everything through the smoky haze. The smoke was worse than being in a serf's hovel, and I ought to know.

John was sitting very upright in a raised chair by the altar. He was in great colourful robes and up high enough so he could be seen through the candle smoke by the huge crowd of nobles and worthies standing in front of him. He seemed to be looking off into the distance without seeing anyone.

Mostly, the onlookers were men, of course, but there were a surprising number of women standing with them in furry robes despite it being a hot summer day and the church being heated by all the candles and people. Most of us were sweating quite large, which made the smell even worse. I did not recognise a single person in the church.

Noticeably absent and the source of much conversation around us was the King's wife, Isabel. I have never seen her, of course, but from the whispered comments I hear whilst we waited for the ceremony to begin there seemed to be some kind of problem.

"She should be here."

"Where is she?"

"Is not she to be queen?"

"No children."

"Cousins, I am told."

After a few minutes there was a great stirring, and the bishop who had been pissing on the church wall next to Thomas marched in behind a priest carrying a golden cross and another holding up a great Bible for everyone to see. A whole long line of loudly chanting priests and bishops followed behind them.

George and the boys ended up being able to see the ceremony better than Thomas and I and most everyone else. They could look over the heads of the crowd and see Hubert put the crown on our new king's head because we lifted them up to stand on the tomb of an old Saxon worthy before the ceremony started.

It was by far the most impressive ceremony I have ever seen. There was a lot of chanting and prayers and exhortations and oaths in Latin from the King, some of which William and I could understand but most of the people around us and the King obviously could not. Then Hubert placed the crown on John's head and we all lustily cheered and clapped our hands for several minutes.

No one paid us the slightest attention as we lifted the boys down off the old tomb and joined the great mass of people who pressed towards the front door to get out into the fresh air. They rushed out after the King left swirling his robes and the bishops and priests marched out chanting their prayers. If anything, those in attendance are probably wondering how people dressed as simply as we are dressed gained admission to such a grand event.

*We joined the people leaving after the ceremony and easily found our wains beyond the crowd assembled in front of the church. None of us saw the King again for some time—not until two years later in Calais, and then I only saw him at a distance when we helped ferry John and some of his army back to England before I sailed for the Holy Land to give the Pope some of the coins from the previous year's offerings by the refugees and pilgrims.*

## Chapter Five
*The Templars bring trouble.*

Our relationship with the Templars and the Pope's other papal orders was tested when William and I returned to Freddy's stable after the ceremony. We found two Templar Knights waiting to see us. They were there, they said, to arrange transportation from London to the Hospitallers' stronghold in Acre for themselves and two others. We, of course, told them we would be pleased to do so.

*That is strange, very strange, indeed; the Templars usually do not have anything to do with the Hospitallers. I wonder why they are going to Acre?*

Our policy towards the Templars and the various other papal orders is quite simple—wherever possible we try to avoid any contact with them. *We want the knights and lords who lead them to make a mistake and seriously underestimate us—and never see us as a competitor for the power and wealth they are constantly pursuing for themselves in the name of "regaining Jerusalem."*

Our policy is to be friendly and distant from the other papal orders. Where we totally differ from the Templars and the other orders is in our effort to conceal the extent to which we are accumulating coins and a powerful military force. In contrast, they are like the Pope and

King—they flaunt their wealth and power in an effort to keep everyone impressed and cowed.

*I think it is because all of their captains are nobles and knights and that was what they learnt from their families when they were young.*

We were not at all like the other orders, of course, and deliberately so; we archers who are 'poor landless sailors' do not make any effort to acquire land or solicit donations except from travellers for the Pope's prayers; the other papal orders do both and do so rather aggressively with threats of damnation and promises of salvation if people touch the relics they claim to possess.

Indeed, last year we signed our Derbyshire lands over to the Templars after old Leslie died and his son was killed in France fighting for King Richard. Our only price was an initial thirty brood mares and a few every year thereafter—which is all we ever wanted from Derbyshire in the first place. Having isolated fiefs scattered around England to pay taxes on and defend and call attention to our wealth may appeal to the Templars, Hospitallers, and Teutonic Knights, but it is not part of our plan for George's future and the future of the archers.

So here's the difference—they use their icons and wealth to impress everyone and acquire even more land; we use our longbows and pikes to remove anyone who tries to stand in our way.

\*\*\*\*\*

Our desire to stay out of sight and mind in England does not mean we do not want or need more property. To the contrary, the main reason William and I are in London today is because we need to station an agent here to represent us—

which means we need some kind of a compound or depot where our agent can safely live and meet merchants to do our business and store our coins before we send them off to Cornwall.

Finding an appropriate place for our port agent near where we moor our galleys and cogs is a problem but not the biggest problem. The biggest problem is finding the right man to be our port agent—because none of our archers know how to scribe and do sums. All we will be able to do until my students are grown is send a dependable man and hire a scribe to assist him.

*****

"Well, Your Eminence, what do you think? It would be a fine place for your man, would not it?"

Freddy's friend Tommy was asking me my opinion about a rather rundown shop space with a rickety ladder going up through a trap door to a room above the shop that could be used as a living quarters and a place to store a coin chest. It is located on a narrow street about two blocks from Freddy's stables and three blocks from the long quay where our galleys are moored. It looks poor and unimpressive.

"I do not know, Tommy, it looks to be in bad shape. If we buy it we would have to spend a lot of coins to fix it up. Besides, there is no alley where the men can pee and poop and no place for the men to cook their bread and meat. They would have to do both out on the street."

*I am negotiating. Actually, it is perfect for our depot because it makes us appear to be poor and would not attract the attention of robbers and the King. On the other hand, the upstairs room will look like a palace to one of our*

*sergeants who has spent most of his life sleeping*
*on the ground or on a rowing bench, and the*
*downstairs room is big enough to sleep the scribe*
*and the four or five archers who will be the post*
*sergeant's guards. One thing we will have to do*
*if we buy it is immediately strengthen the door.*
*Later, we will find a second somewhat similar*
*place nearby we can use as an escape house and*
*dig an escape tunnel to it.*

*****

It was once again raining in London the
next day when William and I and Peter and
Raymond walked from our galleys to take
another look at the empty storefront with the
sleeping room above it. According to Tommy, it
was a linen merchant's shop until its owner and
his wife and children all died of the sweating pox
last summer.

We all crowded into the ground floor room once again and the more we looked at the place the more we liked it. After a bit of bargaining, it came down to ninety-four silver coins and it is ours forever. I nodded to William and he nodded back. Then he dug into the purse he was carrying and paid the price.

William handed the coins to an anxious and obviously relieved older man who swore he is the current owner as the father and only heir of the dead merchant. The seller made his mark on the parchment I hurriedly drafted and accepted the coins as a beaming Tommy stood by. We will record the parchment in the local parish church.

*It is understood by everyone that Tommy will end up with some of the coins. It is also understood that if the old man is not the true*

*owner Tommy himself will return our coins and*
*whatever more we think we deserve for our*
*trouble—or lose his head most painfully.*

\*\*\*\*\*\*

Peter and Raymond and some of the
archers will remain in London to buy more
breeding stock for our horse farm and start the
construction we will require if our new property
is to become a permanent depot. If what we have
done in Constantinople and Rome is any guide,
we will be putting a new wall across the back of
the ground floor room after we buy another
house or shop nearby and the post's guards dig
an escape tunnel to it.

When we finish building the tunnel,
someone who is in the upstairs room at night and
hears robbers or enemies will be able to climb
down into either the main shop or into the new

little room in the back where the escape tunnel will begin.

*I wonder if we have any carpenters and miners among our archers and sailors who would like to spend a few months in London?*

"William, do you and Peter have anyone in mind for our agent in London or know of any carpenters and miners in our ranks?"

\*\*\*\*\*  *Thomas*

Peter and Raymond and their archers will stay in London to buy horses and supervise the work on our new depot after I leave for Rome and William and the boys sail for Cornwall. They will stay in our newly acquired shop and guard the place until a galley from Cornwall returns with whatever men are needed to take their places and complete the work.

When their replacements arrive, Peter, with Raymond as his second, will lead his men and newly acquired horses to Derbyshire where they will get this year's horses from whoever is the Templars' tenant. Then they will travel on through Devon to Cornwall with our new brood mares, fillies, and wagons.

We now have an entire company of what William and the men are starting to call our "horse archers." Raymond is its sergeant captain. Many, and perhaps all, of the men going with Peter are from Raymond's company. Several dozen of them and a smith came with us; they are the archers Peter and Raymond will lead overland to Cornwall.

Our plan is to train more archers to be horse archers and increase the size of Raymond's company as more horses become available. Geldings from our own mares are preferable.

Having companies of highly mobile and thoroughly trained horse archers capable of moving quickly from place to place on horseback and in wagons and horse carts is part of our long-term plan for George's future—and the reason we have been buying fillies and brood mares.

Most men on horseback these days are either lightly armoured cavalry who ride their horses into battle waving swords or heavily armoured knights who ride into battle on the great, huge warhorses called destriers and coursers, the horses the knights tend to ride in their tournaments and battles against other knights.

Neither lightly armoured cavalry nor knights on big horses are much of a match for our archers carrying longbows, and certainly not when our archers are trained to fight and walk in step together as heavy infantry carrying both longbows and bladed pikes.

The problem, of course, is getting heavy infantry and their weapons to where they are needed most to fight effectively—and that is why we are acquiring horses and beginning to train some of our archers to ride and care for them as well as to fight on both land and sea.

We are not old fashioned and stuck in the past like the King and his knights and lords, or the French and the Templars—our horses are mostly for the transportation of supplies and weapons to battlefields and the pulling of carts and ploughs, not for riding in tournaments and battle charges wearing armour the way the knights and nobles do.

Carrying supplies and pulling carts and ploughs is not the only way we intend to use our horses, of course. Raymond's outriders are a good example. They are more like the Saracen Horse we went against in the Holy Land than anything else—fighting men armed with both bows and swords and riding good horses.

No one knows it yet, of course, but as we get more horses, we intend to greatly expand the number of outriders so we can send scouts and entire companies of mounted archers with longbows far beyond Cornwall.

*Keep a couple of steps ahead of the bastards by being better armed and better prepared when we fight is what William is always saying—and what George and the boys are being taught in addition to their sums and scribing.*

# Chapter Six

*We sail for Rome.*

We had found a place for our London shipping post, and it was time to leave. Peter and Raymond and those of our archers who will be going on to Cornwall with the horses stood on the quay and waved as London's morning fog began to lift, and Harold's galley with William and the boys on board slowly rowed off to thread its way through the mass of anchored cogs and ships in the harbour and begin its long run down the channel to Cornwall. Jeffrey's galley bound for Rome with me on board followed closely behind it.

Jeffrey and Harold were not taking any chances in case the weather turns bad and it takes Harold longer than expected to reach Cornwall and Jeffrey to reach Lisbon—both galleys were filled with water skins and flour in barrels and amphora, and both decks were covered with livestock and firewood.

Indeed, the decks of both galleys are so covered with supplies that until some are eaten away the men will have to climb over a struggling and noisy mass of chickens and living and dead sheep to get to the shite nest, which hangs over the rear of each galley.

Every inch of available deck was covered because we have to spread the supplies out to balance the weight; if we stack them too high, the galley will be top heavy and might roll over in a storm. The heaviest supplies, such as the skins and barrels filled with water and flour, of course, go in the deepest part of our not very deep hulls to help hold the galley down in the water so it does not roll over.

***** *Thomas*

Jeffrey ordered our galley to cast off its lines, and we began moving away from the quay at the same time Harold's galley cast and began moving on its voyage to take William and the boys back to Cornwall. We will follow Harold part of the way down the channel towards Cornwall but then veer off to head south on my annual summer voyage to Rome to pay the Pope his share of the contributions from the refugees and pilgrims. It is a long trip; we usually sail with supply stops along the way at ports such as those of Lisbon, Palma, and Bonifacio.

*I am now in Jeffrey's galley because Harold is always the captain whenever George is on a galley or cog. That was why I travelled here on Harold's galley with George and the boys and why, as soon as we arrived in London, I traded places with William and switched my bedding and chamber pot to Jeffrey's galley—and William had his moved to be with the boys in the stern castle of Harold's galley.*

There is no particular hurry to get the coins to the Pope, and we have got two full seventy-man galley companies of archers on board Jeffrey's galley as rowers—so the Pope's coins and I should be quite safe unless the weather catches us out or our pilot runs us aground when the visibility is poor.

And, of course, at each port where we stop for water and supplies, we will be asking around for archers and likely lads to recruit as apprentice archers and for boys who might be capable of learning to scribe and sum. If we find any, we will either bring them on board to sail with us or arrange to collect them when we are on our way back to Cornwall in a month or so.

*****

Lisbon's port was a beehive of activity as we rowed up to the great central quay stretching for miles along the waterfront. The city served by the port was a huge sprawling place many times larger than London. The size of its busy port certainly reflected it.

If anything, Lisbon's port seemed even busier this year than it was when I was here last year on my annual trip to Rome to give the Pope his share of the prayer coins. William stopped here for water and supplies on his way home to

Cornwall earlier this year and said the same thing about it.

*I wonder why the port is so busy? Perhaps the fighting in the interior between the Moslems and Christians is driving people into the city. That anyone would want to come here at all is a bit surprising—it is only been a dozen or so years since a big force of Arab pirates raided Lisbon and took off more than three thousand Christian and Jewish women and children to sell as slaves and use as wives.*

A few minutes after we moored at one of the wooden wharves running off the city's great quay, Jeffrey and I were in the harbour master's office paying our fee for the right to tie up at the wharf for the next seven days. I did not arrive as a bishop. To the contrary, I am wearing my Egyptian tunic with the six stripes of an archer lieutenant over my long chain mail shirt; Jeffrey is also an archer, of course, and his tunic has four stripes as the galley's sergeant captain.

Jeffrey was not wearing chain mail even though he has a chain shirt in our galley's little castle at the front of the galley where we sleep and keep our personal things. Whenever possible I wear my chain shirt under either an archer's tunic or my bishop's robes, and I always wear my wrist knives and either carry a sheathed sword or have one close at hand. *I have had to use them too many times.*

The harbour master was displeased. He twice asked what we were bringing into the city and seemed quite disappointed when he heard we are neither loading nor unloading cargo. His disappointment was obvious as I paid our modest fee for merely mooring temporarily to pick up water, food, and firewood.  It was also understandable—he almost certainly gets a cut of the taxes and fees he collects on cargos coming in and out of the city.

Then Jeffrey and I were truly surprised when the door banged open and Martin Archer bustled into the harbour master's office with a big smile on his face and his hand outstretched to shake ours and pound our backs.  Martin was wearing a rather fancy shirt and skirt instead of the simple archer tunic with the five stripes of a senior sergeant usually worn by all of the original archers.

*Martin relocated last year from Launceston to be our agent in Lisbon with a scribe from Cambridge to write his parchments and tell his lies in Latin.  Apparently, one of the boys who hangs around on the quay near our*

*post had seen our galley arrive and run to get
him.*

Martin showed up so quickly we did not
even have to hire someone to show us the way to
our company depot north of the quay. It is the
depot William bought several years ago with
some of the coins we got by selling some of the
cargo transports he took out of Tunis on our
second big raid. I had visited the depot last year
when I brought the Pope's coins, but I could not
remember the route back to it.

*It is actually quite encouraging for Martin
to show up so quickly. It suggests he has
watchers on the quay to report arriving galleys
and cargo transports and steer potential
travellers and cargos and coin depositors to him.
Is it possible we misjudged him? William will be
pleased when he hears how quickly he arrived.*

Martin's been here for about a year.  He
came from Launceston and, although he does not
know it, he is here because we decided
Launceston needed to be in more dependable
hands—because it is our first and most important
barrier against any hostile forces and clergy
coming against Cornwall by land.

Martin is honest and loyal but, truth be
told, he is sometimes a bit slow and indecisive.
He is here in Rome because we were concerned
he would dither and sit on his hands if an enemy
approached Cornwall instead rushing to hold the
Tamar River ford—or, even worse, he had fall
for some ruse and be gulled into letting an enemy
into Launceston Castle without even putting up a
fight or sending for reinforcements.

*William and I know Launceston Castle is*
*vulnerable and the ford important to hold—*

*because we gulled our way into Launceston*
*ourselves and our archers fought and killed*
*Cornell at the ford when he tried to invade*
*Cornwall.*

The Tamar ford was where we killed
Cornell when he tried to invade Cornwall and
where the Bishop of Cornwall and Devon
crossed into Cornwall to help Henry FitzCount
seize us at Launceston—and got himself gutted
and killed for his trouble, when he and FitzCount
and FitzCount's men thought we were unarmed
because they could not see the wrist knives under
our tunics.

*It is truly surprising England's nobles, and*
*the bishops who are usually some noble's*
*younger son, are so stupid as to think someone*
*born a serf or a churl would only use the*
*weapons the nobles use and only fight as the*

*nobles learn to fight. It bodes well for young*
*George and my students and the future of the*
*archers, it truly does.*

\*\*\*\*\*

Martin, Jeffrey, and I walked to our Lisbon depot as soon as I finished settling with the harbour master for a small moorage fee and the modest bribe Martin took me aside and suggested as appropriate.

Our Lisbon depot is fairly well located in an area of cart wrights and somewhat close to both the harbour and Lisbon's great market. It consists of a small and muddy, walled courtyard with a single tree and a house with one room downstairs, which was once used as some sort of workshop, and a second room upstairs where our treasure chests are kept and Martin lives. He reaches his sleeping and treasure room by climbing a ladder he can pull up at night and in times of danger.

The downstairs room is where the archers guarding the depot sleep and visitors meet with Martin and his scribe to arrange for passages and money orders and the shipment of cargos and messages. Martin's scribe has a quiet, tented place in one of the downstairs corners. I did not recognise him, so I assume he is new to the scribe's position.

We got quite a shock when Martin opened the gate and we walked in with him, at least Jeffery and I did—for waiting for us inside the compound were a number of heavily armed Templars, more than a dozen of them.

The Templars were standing on one side of the compound. On the other side, under the shade of our only tree and watching them rather warily, were four of the six archers who are stationed here permanently as guards and a couple of elderly men who look like merchants waiting to do business with Martin. Another of our archers was standing with the Templars talking to them as we opened the gate and walked in.

Everyone looked up quickly as we entered—and the archer talking to the Templars got a look of guilt on his face when he saw us and scurried back to his fellows. *Uh oh. What is going on here?*

"Martin, did you let them in?" I asked quietly as we smiled and raised our hands in a friendly greeting and the Templars raised theirs and smiled back in response.

"Of course, they are Templars, are not they?"

"Yes, they are.  Of course.  And they are our friends, so you did the right thing by offering them your hospitality."

*But why are so many of them here and inside the walls?  We are badly outnumbered. They could take us right now if they have a mind to do it.  But at least he did not take them inside to foul the place with their smell—they never wash or wipe their arses, you know; trying to live like Jesus and him being the Son of God did not have to do those things.*

"Ah, Bishop Thomas of Cornwall, you've arrived.  We have been waiting for you," an older Templar with a grey beard said, with somewhat of a smile on his face, as he walked over and took my hand and kissed my ring without me even offering it to him.

*His face is smiling but there is no smile in his eyes. Why? And how does he know I am a bishop if I am only wearing the simple tunic of the archers of the Poor Landless Sailors with the six stripes of an archer company lieutenant.*

"I am Pierre of Saint Lo and these are my brother Templars."

"I am honoured to meet you, Sir Pierre," I responded with an acknowledging bow towards him and then his men. "What may a priest of the Holy Father's poor landless sailors do for you and your esteemed fellow Templars?"

"As you may know, we have been fighting here in support of King Sancho's men against the heathen Moors. But now the King has made peace with the Moors and is moving his army further north to fight the Spanish Christians of Leon and Castile and sending young men to study in France even though everything a man needs to know is in the Bible.

"We are on our way to Rome to report the King's heresies.  We are here because we know you stop in Lisbon each year about this time when you are on your way to Rome to see the Holy Father.  We would like to buy passage with you to Rome and pay you to stop in Bonifacio for water and supplies so we can deliver an important message.  We will pay extra for the stop, of course."

"We would be pleased to have you and your Templar brothers travel with us and call in at Bonifacio for our supplies.  Heresies such as education and fighting among Christians must, indeed, be reported to the Holy Father and stopped before they can spread—and the strong arms and weapons of you and your Templar brothers will be a welcome addition to our own if we encounter pirates or Moors along the way."

*It is all ox shite, of course, about it being a heresy for a man to know more than just the words in the Bible or to fight off foreign invaders when they claim to be Christians. I am just gulling the Templar by telling him what he wants to hear. We need to be careful around this man; he is dangerous for sure. I do not know why but I can feel it.*

***** *Thomas*

Twenty-two Templars will be on board with us when we sail. Having the Templars on board means, I informed Jeffrey loudly enough so the Templars could hear, we will be stopping in Ibiza to replenish our stores instead of going all the way to Palma. From Ibiza, depending on the weather and winds, we will sail on to

Bonifacio for another supply stop before we sail on the final leg of our voyage to Rome.

*I said it loudly because I wanted the Templars to know we will only be stopping in Ibiza because they will be on board. In fact, with the Templars as passengers, we would not have gone to Palma and might well have stopped in Ibiza even if they had not requested it. I want to sweeten the Templars, but I do not want them to see how our depot operates in Palma or the defences we have in place to keep out thieves and enemies. They have already learnt too much here as it is.*

More important than where we stop, at least to me since the Templars are so opposed to education, "since everything one needs to know is in the Bible," I decided to make no effort in

Lisbon or anywhere else to find any likely lads to join my students in Cornwall.

I also quickly took Martin aside and told him not to sell any passages or parchment money orders to go on Jeffrey's galley because we cannot carry any more than our crew and the twenty or so Templars without overloading the galley and running out of food and water.

Jeffrey started to correct me by saying that we have room for more—but he saw the hard look I gave him as he started to open his mouth and quickly agreed with me about the need to stop for supplies before we get to Palma.

"Aye. You are right, Thomas; yes, you are. We cannot take the risk of being overloaded or running out of water—particularly not if we are carrying Templars to Rome on an important mission for the Pope."

*A fear of overloading the galley and running out of water is not the reason for my order and Jeffrey knows it. I told Martin not to sell passages because I do not want the Templars to see the number of coins that flow to us from our post in Palma or how we protect them. I do not know why but I have a bad feeling about our passengers and their leader.*

Later, before we walk back to the galley, I quietly took Jeffrey aside to share my concerns about the Templars and give him instructions as to what I want him to do next.

"Send a man back to the galley. Have him tell the men we will be heading into pirate waters from here and you will be holding an inspection as soon as we get back from eating at the tavern and that you expect to see every archer with his bow and a quiver of arrows on the peg next to his bench and a shield and sword under his rowing bench—and that the men who do not have them in place when you inspect would not be getting any shore leave to drink too much ale and dip their dingles in the local girls."

# Chapter Seven

*We are dragged into a dispute.*

Two days later we were fully resupplied, the rowing drum began its beat, and we slowly rowed out of Lisbon's great harbour bound for the Mediterranean with stops at Ibiza, Bonifacio, and Rome if all goes well and the weather cooperates. The sea was calm, and the wind and weather look favourable—and even before we cleared the harbour, the Templars were getting sea poxed and crowding the deck railings to the loudly announced disgust of the archers whose oars are below them and will sooner or later have to be shipped and cleaned.

The Templars behaved themselves and even helped us row in order to speed us along. All went well until we reached Bonifacio, the little port city at the southern tip of Corsica. *It is a Christian city with a Byzantine governor and Orthodox churches. It is quite insignificant because Corsica is insignificant.*

Then everything changed—for the very first thing the Templars did upon entering the city was provoke its citizens by attacking a Byzantine priest in the market.

It happened as soon as we arrived. Jeffrey was with me, and we were just coming out of the tax collector's office inside the city walls after paying our mooring fees when one of Jeffrey's sergeants, the one in charge of his sailors, rushed in all out of breath to report trouble, big trouble.

He had been in the city market buying supplies and seen it all.

"Just walked up to the priest and cut him down with his sword. That is what the Templar done. Never seen the likes of it in me whole life, have I?

"Orrible, it was; just orrible. The priest was just walking along minding his own business. Did not say a word, did he, the Templar, I mean. He just up and cut the poor sod down?"

"Back to the galley," was my immediate response as Jeffrey and I looked at each other in amazement.

"This is no quarrel of ours. What is the state of our water and food, Jeffrey?" I asked as we began hurrying back to the galley.

*Then it struck me. My God. We brought the Templars here. The Byzantines the Orthodox priests will blame us.*

We could hear a loud and growing rumble of noise behind us as we walked rapidly back toward the quay. People on the street were alert and rapidly becoming fewer and fewer in number as we hurried along. Window shutters were being closed and doors barred.

Many of the men we met as we hurried along the narrow street were standing in front of their homes and shops. They had armed themselves and obviously intended to protect their properties. They looked at us with questions in their eyes and some of them hailed us as we walked rapidly back to the galley. We instinctively responded with friendly shoulder shrugs, raised eyebrows, and hand gestures indicating "we do not know what the hell is going on and it worries us too" as we hurried past them without stopping.

Even more alarming, men were coming past us carrying weapons and moving towards the noise growing behind us. So were a large and rapidly growing number of young boys.

From what I could see, most of the people on the street were like us—they do not know what the hell is going on and do not intend to wait around to find out.

Suddenly, the noise increased and the Templars came running down the street behind us—and obviously going towards the same city gate opening on to the quay where we were headed—and behind them there was a huge mob of rock-throwing and shouting young men and boys. They were angry and totally out of control; some of them were brandishing weapons.

"Hurry," I shouted to Jeffrey and the four archers who were with us. "Run for the galley, goddamn it. Run. This is no place for us." *What the hell is going on here?*

\*\*\*\*\*

We reached our galley and I literally jumped aboard without breaking stride as Jeffrey headed straight for the fore and aft mooring lines. The first of the Templars jumped on right behind me and joined me in taking a tumble as he did. *It is a pity he did not break his goddamn neck; I am angry about our being made to appear to be involved in whatever happened.*

Jeffrey himself threw one line off and then ran down the quay and threw off the other. *Damn it; the archers and I should have should have stopped to help him.* Then Jeffrey jumped on to the deck of his galley as it slowly drifted away from the quay—and drifted far enough out away from the quay to leave about half of the Templars unable to jump aboard. We watched as they turned to fight the mob and our men poured on deck with their arms. *Well, hell; we cannot leave them even if I had damn well like to do.*

"Lower deck men, man the oars," Jeffery roared out in a great shout. "Hold your arrows. Do not launch. We are bringing her back to the quay to pick up the Templars."

*I am almost tempted to tell Jeffrey to leave the Templars to the fate they have earned—and I would if I were absolutely sure that is the right thing to do. But I am not. What the hell is going on here?*

The Templars who arrived on the quay too late to jump on board were in a group facing the hostile crowd with their swords drawn and their backs to the water. Our oars made a tentative start and then slowly moved the galley back up against the quay.

There were a dozen or so Templars on the quay. They had seen us coming and began jumping on to the galley's deck as soon as we bumped up against it.

One of them seemed to be injured, probably by a rock hitting his head. There was no time for niceties—he was literally picked up and thrown on board by a couple of his fellow Templars.

A few seconds after the injured Templar landed on the deck with a thump, we pushed off from the quay with our bladed pikes and pulled away from it.  A hail of rocks followed us as the mob surged forward.  The last of the Templars, the two who picked up the injured man and threw him aboard, jumped down onto our galley's deck as the archers and sailors with pikes pushed us off.

"Sir Pierre, where are you?" I roared amongst all the shouting and confusion.  I am absolutely furious and rightly so.

*****

A few seconds later, a red-faced and wheezing Sir Pierre made his way across the crowded deck towards me.  He had one of the last two Templars who jumped aboard.

"What was that all about?  Did one of your men really cut down an Orthodox priest in the market?"

"I do not know, Bishop. I really do not."

*He is a goddamn liar. I can see it in his eyes and I know it from what Jeffrey's sailing sergeant told us. But why did he do it, and what should I do now?*

"Jeffrey, are all of our men on board?" I asked our galley's anxious captain. "Have your sergeants make an immediate count of their men, please. We are not leaving anyone behind even if we have to go back and fight the bastards."

*I spoke quite loudly so our men and the Templars could hear. Of course, I did.*

\*\*\*\*\*

A few pulls on the oars was all it took to move us far enough away from the quay to escape the rocks the young men were throwing at us. I would have had Jeffrey immediately row us out of the harbour without trying to resolve the matter except then we would be short of both water and food supplies. So I said nothing and we waited whilst the crowd on the quay continued to grow.

After about an hour later, a dinghy was lowered from one of the cogs moored along the quay. There was a sailor man at the oars and a single passenger. They rowed toward us and stopped just out of hailing distance; the passenger waved and I made an acknowledging wave back.

"Bring our dinghy alongside, Jeffrey, with a good ferryman on the oars. I will go talk to them."

I took off my tunic, shed my chain mail, and put my tunic back on; then I kicked off my sandals, stepped over the galley's rail, and gingerly climbed down into Jeffrey's dinghy with a couple of Jeffrey's sailors steadying me so I would not fall.

*I learnt to swim in the river that ran past the village when I was a boy but I was never very good at it. Everyone says it is particularly hard to do when you are wearing armour and sandals. I do not want to find out.*

Our would-be visitor's dinghy had stopped and waited for me well away from our galley. He made an acknowledging gesture when he saw me start to climb down into our dinghy. I cannot say I blame him for being cautious. I certainly would be if our positions were reversed.

"Hello. Who are you?" he hailed first in Italian and then in Latin as we approached.

"I am Herman von Neurath," I replied in French. "Captain of the Valkrie out of Frankfurt.

Carrying a party of Teutonic Knights from Frankfurt to Beirut to join the crusade. Who are you?"

*Of course, I lied about who I am. So would you under the circumstances. Maybe I can blame this disaster on the Teutonic Knights if they did not catch any of the Templars or our crew. We do not have any dealings with the Teutonic Knights, you know.*

"I am Valens, the son of Joseph," he replied in bad French. "I am the commander of the city watch. Bishop Bardas sent me to find out why our priests were murdered and bring the murderers to him for justice."

*Damn. There were more priests than just the one and they died. That will make settling things down all the more difficult.*

"Priests? Priests were murdered? More than one? That is terrible. Very terrible. What happened? Can you tell me what happened? We just arrived. All I know is I was walking back to my galley from paying the mooring fee at the harbour office with some of my men when a mob started chasing us and throwing rocks."

"Yes, priests were murdered; Father Apostos and several others. Father Apostos was the first. A crusader with a sword cut him down in the market in front of the church.

"People say it was a Templar who did it, and for no reason at all. None. And in the fighting that followed, he and other Templar Knights killed seven more people and wounded a dozen more."

"Priests and innocents? How horrible," I said as I crossed myself. *I really meant it.*

"The murderers will surely rot in hell," I said. "What happened? Was there an argument?"

"We are not sure. Will you bring your galley back to the quay so we can talk to the knights?"

"Yes, of course, that is the correct thing to do; of course, it is. I will ask the commander of the knights who chartered us if he will allow it. I hope he agrees. Will you wait here whilst I speak with him?"

*Sir Pierre would not agree, of course, but I am trying to be as pleasant and obliging as possible under the circumstances. We may want to call in here again sometime and be welcome when we do. Fat chance of that, eh?*

*****

I was hungry so I had a bowl of wine and ate a flatbread and some cheese whilst I was supposedly talking to the leader of the Teutonic Knights.

Twenty minutes later, I climbed back into the galley's dinghy and once again Jeffrey's sailor rowed me back to where the commander of the city watch was bobbing up and down waiting for me to return.

Whilst I was away to "talk to the Teutonic Knights," I had watched a second dinghy come out to the watch commander's dinghy and then row back to one of the cargo transports moored against the quay.

The only good news as I went to my second meeting with the commander of the city watch is that none of our men and none of the Templars are missing. *I had seen the messenger come out to watch the commander whilst I was eating. As we approached the commander, I was wondering what he now knows that I do not.*

"I am sorry, my friend, the commander of the Teutonic Knights refuses. He saw the mob and does not want any more fighting. I would bring my galley and the knights back to the quay myself but there are too many of the Teutonic Knights and their men on board. I am afraid they will take over my galley and kill me if I anger them."

"I thought that might be the knight's answer. Whilst you were aboard your galley, I received more information. There are eight dead in the attack on the Church and three of them are priests. Many others are wounded including two priests, one of whom will almost certainly die.

"Everyone who saw the attacks on the priests says their murderers were Latins, the Pope's Templars for sure." *They think it was an attack on the Orthodox Church by the Pope's men?  This is serious.*

"How can that be?  Most of my passengers are knights of the Teutonic Order and their squires and servants.  It does not make sense.  Why would they pretend to be Templars and do such a thing?"

*I know they are not Teutonic Knights but why did the Templars do it?  It does not make sense—or does it?*

\*\*\*\*\*

"There is no sense staying here any longer.  There is no way we are going to get water and supplies without giving up the Templars."

That was what I told an anxious Jeffrey after his sailor rowed me back to our galley. The Templars standing nearby heard me and seemed quite pleased.

# Chapter Eight

*Forced to flee.*

We left Ibiza quickly. The commander of
the city watch was still climbing out of his
dinghy when the rowing drum of our galley
began its beat and we rowed out of the harbour
with all the Templars on board—and we left
without anywhere near enough of the water we
will need for the final leg of our voyage. We
probably have enough food and firewood for
cooking to reach Rome if we go on half rations,
but not nearly enough water, goddamn it.

There is nothing to do but tighten our belts
and continue north along the Corsican coast until

we come to a usable stream and can use our leather buckets to dip up the water we need to fill our barrels and skins.

According to Jeffrey's map there is a small city with a port about thirty miles up the coast. It is probably just a poor fishing village but it should have some sort of water supply running past it. Hopefully, we will find a suitable stream before we reach it.

***** *Jeffrey and Thomas*

"I have had a couple of my most dependable men listening to the Templars as you requested, Thomas. There is no question about it—they are quite pleased with how things turned out. Not just that they escaped without losing anyone, mind you—they are happy about the fighting and about the dead priests.

"Strangely enough, they have not been talking about why they did it, although, they do seem to appreciate that you tried to protect their order's reputation by telling the Corsicans their attackers were Teutonic Knights."

Jeffrey then paused whilst he tried to figure how he could best say what he wanted to say next.

"It is understandable that the Templars are not upset about you trying to protect them, mind you, but I would have thought they would have been more forthcoming about what happened and why. Soldiers tend to be excited and talk a lot right after a battle, do not they? These did not."

*Jeffrey thinks they have been ordered not to talk even before the murders were committed. He may be right. But why did they do it? What do the Templars have to hide?*

"Well, it had to be done, me suggesting to the Corsicans it was the Teutonic Knights who killed their priests. We always try to help the Templars whenever we can even if we are poor and not associated with their order. That is why we are carrying them to Rome."

*I said it loud enough for some of the Templars and our men to hear. The word will spread, and I want the Templars to know we mean them no harm. This lot we can handle but we are sure to run into a lot more of them sooner or later. The damn Templars are everywhere and their strength and wealth is growing fast, as everyone can see—but not as fast as ours, as everyone cannot see.*

***** *Thomas*

We did not start towards Rome as quickly as I had hoped we might. It took the rest of the day to row along the coast and find a stream where we could dip our buckets and pull up enough fresh water to refill our barrels and water skins. Then that night a storm blew us well south of the mouth of River Tibor before our pilot realised where we were and turned us back north.

It took two days of hard rowing against the wind to move far enough northward—but in the end, and totally out of food and firewood for cooking our flatbread, we finally reached the mouth of the River Tibor and rowed up the river to Rome's crowded wharves.

Everyone was hungry from being on half rations, so the first thing we did was hand out copper coins and let our sailors and archers go to the shops and stalls along the wharf to buy bread and olives and drink a bowl of wine.

The Templars quickly disappeared. Their order has an impressive, large building and a significant number of men here in Rome, so it was not surprising at all when they hurried away. What was a bit surprising was they did so without so much as a word of thanks or a farewell wave—and to add insult to injury, the arrogant bastards did not pay us.

\*\*\*\*\*

Rome is Rome and a splendid walled city it is. Everywhere there are great buildings, large markets, and ancient ruins and monuments. Within the city walls there are several hundred fortified residential towers, mini-castles erected by the city's various leading families and religious organisations to provide protection against their enemies and proclaim their high status and great riches. The Templars' flag flies over one of the largest and richest of them all.

I thought about taking off all my clothes, putting on my bishop's robe and mitre, and walking to our depot. But I did not; it is too damn warm to walk anywhere under the hot Roman sun dressed in my bishop's robe and mitre. Instead, I left my archer's tunic on and, after fortifying myself with a visit to a food stall for a chicken leg and a bowl of wine, I walked to our depot with a large guard of archers.

Our depot is not nearly as impressive as the Templars' great fortress, just a shabby fortified compound and rundown tower on the Via Margutta. Two dozen heavily armed archers accompanied me. The depot gate was barred, but an eye appeared at a viewing hole and the gate opened when the sergeant commanding my guard of archers announced our arrival by using the handle of his sword to pound on the little door within the larger gate.

*It is good to see precautions being taken. The city is reputed to becoming quite dangerous now that a commune representing the city's powerful families is running it instead of one of the Pope's cardinals and their priests. I was halfway to the depot when I realised I was not wearing my chain mail shirt—and began wondering if I had not made a mistake.*

*One can only wonder how long the peace will last before the Pope tries to regain control of the entire city—and if the Church is not deliberately starting the attacks and riots to encourage the commune to surrender its power.*

Randolph came running out to the gate to meet me and we fell into each other's arms as only old soldiers do after they have stood side by side in numerous battles. The archers both here and in my guard were strangely pleased by the warmth of our reunion.

Yes, it is Randolph from Constantinople, one of the original archers and the man William considers to be our single most dependable sergeant—and I could not agree more.

William moved Randolph from Constantinople to Rome to command our shipping depot here. He moved him following our unfortunate misunderstanding with the Byzantines which resulted, as everyone now knows, when Randolph and some of his men were captured in Constantinople by some of the Emperor's men and held for ransom.

William refused to pay the ransom, of course. Instead, he surprised the Byzantines by mobilising all of our available archers and giving their Emperor a choice between either producing Randolph and our men alive, or having his city burned, his army destroyed, and his fleet sunk.

*My brother did the right thing in going to Randolph's rescue and it brought great relief to our men who have a justifiable fear, as all soldiers do, of being abandoned by their commanders. It happens all too frequently and they know it. Look at Richard, for God's sake.*

The Byzantine emperor in Constantinople saw the size of our force of archers and did not initially take William's threat seriously when he compared it to the size of his own army. He finally saw the light, and "came to Jesus" as the popular saying goes in the monasteries, but only after William and his archers came up from Cyprus and promptly sailed off with a good part of the Byzantine fleet as prizes and then killed a large number of the Emperor's best men in several days of fighting in front of Constantinople's walls.

It took a few days of serious fighting but the Emperor ultimately saw the wisdom of blaming others for causing the problem and had Randolph and his men released. Even better, the Emperor compensated us for our troubles. As a result, Randolph is now in Rome to get him away from any possible retribution by the damn Greeks and we now have a permanent post and mooring spaces in Constantinople and more chests of coins in Cornwall.

Long Bob replaced Randolph and seems to be doing quite well in Constantinople. The Byzantine galleys and cargo transports we took as prizes were either sold or added to our fleet and every one of our men, all the way down to the former slaves who helped us row, received serious prize monies from their capture.

In other words, Constantinople worked out quite nicely for us after Randolph got captured except for those of our men who got killed or permanently injured—and they are not bothering anyone because they are out of sight and mind either in their graves or comfortably retired on loan lands with enough coins to see them out.

"It is good to see you here and safe, it truly is," I said to Randolph for the second or third time as I lifted my bowl of wine in salute.

# Chapter Nine

*Correcting the Pope.*

Randolph and I spent the rest of the day and evening drinking good wine, eating flat bread with melted cheese and sliced meat on it, and reminiscing about our battles and all the archers who sailed with Richard those many years ago. Even between us we could not remember all their names or where they fell.

Fairly early the next morning I put on my bishop's robe, place my mitre firmly on my head, and set off for the Pope's residence carrying my crozier and the bag purporting to contain all the coins the refugees and pilgrims paid to buy the

Pope's goodwill and prayers. Randolph and Jeffrey came with me.

I was not wearing my chain mail or my wrist knives, but I was surrounded front and back by more than a dozen archers carrying both swords and longbows. We were out starting early because the weather in Rome is getting warm. Hopefully, the Pope will be done with his prayers by the time we reach his residence.

"The city is no longer safe since the commune took over," Randolph observed when he insisted on so many guards accompanying us. "Not even the Pope is safe and you are only a poor bishop."

We walked in the hot morning sun, and I was sweating and overly warm in my bishop's robe when Randolph and I reached the gate one must use to enter the Pope's own walled minicity within the great city walls of Rome. This is my second visit to carry coins to the new Pope, so I knew where to go and what to expect.

\*\*\*\*\*

By far the grandest of all the districts in Rome is the walled area in the centre of the city where the Pope resides and the Church conducts its business. They have made it grand, so it is said, to impress people with the Church's wealth and power.

I walked to the Pope's palace in the already-hot, summer morning sun with a party of archers to protect my person and the little sack of gold and silver coins containing this year's payment of the coins the pilgrims and refugees paid to buy the Pope's prayers for the safety of their voyage.

The guard at the papal gate was fairly alert and greeted me quite cordially in Latin as is appropriate since I was wearing my mitre and carrying my crozier. He seemed to expect me, although, perhaps I am just imagining it. Or, perhaps, my arrival with so many guards encouraged him to believe I am someone sufficiently important, to be treated properly.

In any event, one of the three young priests loitering behind the guard in the little guard house courteously welcomed me and pointed out a shady spot where Randolph and Jeffrey and my guards can wait for my return and the little alcove set into the wall where they can relieve themselves if they so require.

He will, the priest volunteered, send out some good water and melon slices for my men to help them fight off the heat.  I thanked him profusely for the kindness and so did Randolph.

\*\*\*\*\*

My guide walked ahead of me and said not a word as we crossed the cobblestoned square and entered the long, low building serving as the entrance to the Pope's quarters and the offices of the worldwide church.  It was quiet as we walked down the flagstone corridor, although, I could hear murmurs of voices in the rooms we pass, and several times I caught sight of priests and bishops sitting on stools in front of writing desks and on benches along the walls.

I have never been quite sure what this building is—probably the guardroom and some of the minor administrative offices.  It seems to stand between the street and the building housing the Pope's residence and the Church's treasury.  I wish I knew so I could tell George and the boys for when they are the ones making the trip.

"Ah, Bishop Thomas, it is good to see you once again. I am sure His Holiness will be pleased to see you as well. Please, lift your arms. . . ."

What followed was a thorough inspection of my person and robes to make sure I was not carrying weapons. I am not carrying any, of course, not even my wrist knives. It went quickly.

*As usual, no one checked my wrists when I raised my hands high over my head. I considered saying something but decided not to; you never know, do you?*

"Thank you, Bishop. I am sure you understand our need to be careful. Please follow Father Alberto. He will take you to the papal chambers.  I will wait here and accompany you back to your men after your reception.  There is a door over there that goes to an outside alley if you need to relieve yourself before meeting the Holy Father."

\*\*\*\*\*

Innocent III is a sturdy and surprisingly young man and this was not my first visit to deliver our tribute.  He rose with a smile as I entered and held out his ring for me to kiss whilst gesturing with his other hand for me to put the pouch of coins on the table next to his chair.

*He probably needs the money.  Rumour is his family had to spend forty mule-loads of gold to buy enough votes for his appointment.  But he is canny; yes, he is.  It is no wonder his family made the investment.  I wonder who loaned his family all that gold and what they had to promise to get it?*

"Bishop Thomas. Welcome once again and God's blessing on you. I hope my prayers for our pilgrims and refugees have been helpful?"

"Oh, they have, Holy Father, they have indeed. I am sure of it."

Then our talk turned serious and the Pope began questioning me with several priests hovering in the background—and attempting to listen without appearing to do so. They looked young and fit.

"They tell me you have just been in Corsica. What do you know of the attacks the Orthodox priests and their followers made on the Templars and our own Christian people?"

"There were problems in Corsica whilst we were there taking on food and water but I know of no such attacks on our people, Your Holiness. If anything, it was the other way around—although, of course, attacks on our people might have occurred afterwards without me knowing about them." *Damn. What does he want to hear, and what should I tell him?*

"I was told you stopped in Corsica on your way here carrying the tithes from the pilgrims and were attacked by Orthodox priests as were the Templars traveling with you. Is that not true?"

"Not exactly, Your Holiness. In fact, it is not true at all—although it is true that whilst I was in Corsica there was an incident involving the Templars and an Orthodox priest. One of my men happened to be in the market buying supplies and saw the whole thing."

I told the Holy Father the entire story including how it came to be I was sailing with the Templars.

It took quite some time to tell the story because the Holy Father asked many questions about what happened in Corsica after the Templars killed the priest and what different people did and why. He seemed to be increasingly distressed at what he was hearing.

*Why is he so distressed? Did someone tell him the Templars were attacked? Why would they do that?*

Then the Holy Father asked me to tell him what I know about the fighting that occurred last year at Constantinople between our archers, the men he knows as the 'Order of poor Landless Sailors,' and the Byzantine troops.

He seemed particularly surprised when I explained the attack by the Emperor's troops occurred as a result of William's response to a ransom demand by some of the Emperor's people—and that it had absolutely nothing to do with Emperor Alexios and the Orthodox Patriarch trying to prevent the 'Poor Landless Sailors' from helping to carry the crusaders of the current crusade to the Holy Land to free Jerusalem. *Where could he have gotten such an idea?*

"Do you think," His Holiness asked whilst looking at me most intently, "the Byzantines are in league with the Saracens such that our crusaders must capture Constantinople before they can recapture Jerusalem?"

"I find that hard to believe, Your Holiness; very hard, indeed. Impossible, actually. We have a post in Constantinople and I am sure we would have quickly heard about such a relationship if it existed. It does not make sense; it cannot be true."

*Although, it certainly would be good for our coin chests if the crusaders do try to take Constantinople—there would be many refugees and money transfers.*

*****

I had much to think about as I followed a young priest back to the entrance gate to join Randolph and Jeffrey and my guards. They had been waiting patiently in the shade and scrambled to their feet as we approached.

There is no doubt in my mind, and apparently not in the Pope's mind either—the

Templars and the crusaders now on their way to the Holy Land by the Venetians are playing some sort of dangerous game. But what is it and why?

*Actually, I think I know what is driving the crusaders and so does the Pope; although, perhaps he does not want to admit it. In reality, most crusaders do not answer a Pope's call and go on a crusade for religious reasons. They go in hopes of enriching themselves—and the current crusaders may be looking for other cities to conquer because the early crusades proved there is not much gold in Jerusalem or viable land around it. But what will the Pope do and the crusaders do and how should William and I respond?*

# Chapter Ten

*The Pope sets a task.*

Within an hour of my returning to our depot near the Tibor wharf, a rotund little cardinal with a big smile arrived with a parchment letter sealed with a papal seal. He handed it to me without a word and waited silently whilst I read it. It was a message to me from the Pope and explained why Cardinal Antonio Bertoli arrived at our door in the company of a large number of papal guards.

"In the name of God, I command you and your fellow Englishmen to immediately carry Cardinal Bertoli to Venice on an important mission. It is a matter of great importance and he must leave with you immediately or else his life and his mission will be in danger."

*Venice? That is where the crusaders are gathering to go on the Pope's new crusade. And why is his life in danger?*

"Uh. Cardinal Bertoli, the Holy Father seems to think that your mission and your life may be in danger. Why might that be?"

\*\*\*\*\*

Bertoli explained that the Pope's order for us to take him to Venice is in regards to the crusade Pope Innocent called to arms last year to recapture Jerusalem. It will be the Fourth Crusade and second such effort to retake Jerusalem since it was lost to the Saracens.

*Lost, I reminded myself as I listened to Cardinal Bertoli's explanation, due to the military stupidity of the man who was then Jerusalem's king—King Guy; the same King Guy who is now the King of Cyprus where we base our men and galleys serving the Holy Land and other Mediterranean ports.*

It seems Cardinal Bertoli has been sent to me by the Pope because I have a galley immediately available and he has an important papal letter to deliver to the Pope's ambassador to the crusaders. The ambassador is a cardinal and, of course, an Italian. His name is Peter of Capua. The latest word, according to Cardinal Bertoli, suggests Cardinal Capua is with the crusaders assembling in Venice.

I tried to be enthusiastic about helping the Cardinal deliver the Pope's letter even though I would have much preferred to return directly to England. *Truth be told, I regret I did not go straight to the galley and sail immediately. Giving the Pope time to come up with something for me to do was a mistake I would not make again.*

"Of course, I will do everything possible to assist the Pope and the crusaders. Last time, King Richard got to within twenty miles of Jerusalem. This time, I am sure the crusaders will regain the city."

*I am not at all sure they will be successful, but that is what the Cardinal expected me to say.*

Sailing all the way down the coast of Italy and back up the other side to Venice to deliver the Pope's letter will take more than a week even if the winds are favourable—but not as many days as it would take for Cardinal Bertoli to travel by mule or horse cart all the way to Venice by land or to travel overland across Italy and catch a galley bound for Venice from one of the Italian ports on the Adriatic Sea.

There is no doubt about it—sailing from Rome in a well-manned galley such as Jeffrey's is the fastest way for Cardinal Bertoli to get to Venice and deliver the Pope's letter.

\*\*\*\*\*

Cardinal Bertoli wanted to sail as quickly as possible and, after a bit of prodding, he explained why.

Word has reached Rome that the Venetian ruler, the Doge, has given the impoverished crusaders a way to get the coins they need to pay for their transportation to the Holy Land—by collecting the taxes and fees Venice claims it is due from Zara and several smaller Adriatic port cities that broke away from Venice about twenty years ago and aligned themselves with the Kingdom of Hungary and its Orthodox king and church.

It seems the Venetians have "contributed" the uncollected revenues for those twenty years to the crusade and are offering to carry the crusaders to the Adriatic ports to collect them, by force if necessary, so the crusaders can pay for their transportation to Egypt and from there to Jerusalem's port of Acre, which is still being held by the Hospitallers.

Venice's proposal is a problem for the Pope, according to Bertoli, because Zara and the other Adriatic port cities across from Italy are Christian cities, albeit Orthodox, and Innocent III does not want "his" crusade to cause fighting between Christians. As a result, Bertoli is carrying an important letter from the Pope to Cardinal Peter of Capua, the man who is with the crusaders as the Pope's legate.

The Pope's letter is quite specific, said Bertoli—it instructs Cardinal Capua to inform the crusaders His Holiness will excommunicate any crusader who attacks any of his fellow Christians, even Orthodox Christians.

"Unfortunately," Bertoli said with a great sigh and a shrug of resignation, "what the Pope's letter does not do is tell the crusade's leaders how they are to get the coins they need to hire the Venetian galleys and transports to carry their men and horses to the Holy Land."

\*\*\*\*\*

Cardinal Bertoli and I spent a lot of time talking a lot during our twelve-day voyage to

Venice. It helped distract me from being sea poxed and I learnt a lot.

It seems the crusade Pope Innocent has called, the fourth crusade as it is now named, will be conducted more like Richard's almost successful third crusade than the first two crusades—it will go to the Holy Land by sea from Venice via Egypt and Acre instead of marching overland from Constantinople along the increasingly dangerous route travelled by the first two crusades.

According to Cardinal Bertoli, the Fourth Crusade will be leaving from Venice because the elderly and now-blind Doge who rules seafaring Venice is the only one willing to provide enough transports and galleys to carry the crusaders to a staging area in Egypt and then on to Acre.

*Hmm. I wonder why they did not ask us to carry them? Not that we would have agreed, of course—because crusaders are notorious for not paying.*

Acre is a good place for the crusaders to land because it is the port of Jerusalem and one of the few ports in the Holy Land still held by Christian knights—the Hospitallers from whom we had bought the weapons of the three thousand Saracens Richard murdered after they surrendered.

The crusaders, and thus Pope Innocent because he is the man who called for the crusade on behalf of God and wanted it to succeed, have a serious problem according to Cardinal Bertoli. No country except Venice has enough sailors and cargo transports to carry the crusaders to Egypt and the Holy Land and is also willing to do so—

and the crusaders do not have sufficient coins to pay the Venetians.

*****

We sailed immediately from Rome and went all the way around the boot of Italy and back up the other side to Venice. There was good news when we arrived in Venice and Cardinal Bertoli was visibly relieved when he heard it.

It seems that even though a few of the crusaders have sailed for the Adriatic ports to try to collect the back taxes Venice claims it is owed, most of them are still here in Venice—they have not yet sailed off to threaten or attack the Christian ports.

There was other news which was not so good—the Pope's legate, his ambassador to the crusaders, was not in Venice to receive the

Pope's letter. Cardinal Peter of Capua sailed for Pula and various other port cities on the Adriatic two days earlier to seek their voluntary payment of the uncollected taxes Venice has donated to the crusade.

According to whomever Cardinal Bertoli spoke with, a bishop whose name I had never heard before, Cardinal Capua has gone to ask Pula and the other port cities to voluntarily help pay for the crusaders' transportation to the Holy Land in order to avoid the shedding of Christian blood.

Capua's departure, of course, is quite inconvenient because it means we will have to carry Cardinal Bertoli to Pula or elsewhere to deliver the Pope's letter.

*****

What we did not know, and no one in Venice told us when we arrived, was that someone in Rome had betrayed the Pope by sending a galloper across Italy to catch a galley at Pescara—and he had gotten to Venice ahead of us with a message warning the Venetians and crusaders about the Pope's letter.

For the Venetians, the issue is simple— they want the money the crusaders have agreed to pay them to be carried to Egypt and the Holy Land—and they want the crusaders to get it by teaching Zara and the other Christian ports a lesson about the folly of looking to Hungary's king to protect them instead of Venice.

We, of course, knew nothing of any of this when we sailed out of Venice in pursuit of the Pope's legate—we were following Cardinal Capua to Zara not knowing that the Venetian galleys who had left the harbour a few hours before we sailed had been ordered to prevent us from delivering the Pope's letter.

# Chapter Eleven

*Our arrival causes problems.*

Venice is a large and important city.
Cargo transports and galleys have been
constantly coming and going from Venice's huge
and crowded harbour ever since we arrived in
Venice this morning and Cardinal Bertoli hurried
off to the residence of the local papal nuncio with
an escort of guards from Jeffrey's archers.

The Cardinal's rapid return less than an
hour later resulted in Jeffrey recalling his
disappointed men from the local taverns and

whorehouses and speeding up our taking on of water and supplies.

*I am not at all happy about having to leave Venice so quickly and neither are our archers and sailors—I was looking forward to a cup of wine in one of the taverns I had heard about and then going home.  I have already been away from George and the boys longer than I expected.*

My personal distress at leaving so soon meant nothing.  Less than four hours after we moored on the Venetian quay, Jeffrey's rowing drum began to beat and we rowed rapidly out of Venice's crowded and filthy harbour bound for someplace called Pula.

We rowed away from the quay with great, billowing, white clouds overhead, pigeons and seagulls everywhere, a great deal of garbage and debris in the water including dead animals and at least one extremely white and bloated body. No one on board, not even Jeffrey's pilot, knows much about Pula except that it is a little port further down the coast.

All we know is the Venetians claim Pula owes them taxes and that the taxes now belong to the crusaders. As a city, Pula is so inconsequential even Jeffrey's pilot had never visited it. We left Venice so quickly that several of Jeffrey's men were left behind.

Venice is one of the world's busiest ports with cargo transports and war galleys constantly arriving and leaving. We thought nothing of it when we watched a number of Venetian galleys leave the great city's crowded and stinking harbour ahead of us and head off in the same general direction we are heading with our sail up and our rowing benches fully manned.

\*\*\*\*\*

"There certainly are a large number of galleys out here, Jeffrey. I am not used to seeing so many galleys this far from shore."

"You are right about that, Thomas; yes, you are. But it is to be expected, is not it? Venice is one of the biggest ports in the world and it is got the largest fleet of cogs and other cargo transports. Even bigger than Genoa's, is not it? More war galleys than anyone else too, for that matter. It is got the most powerful navy in the world, does not it?"

*Jeffrey's wrong about the size of the Venetian fleet, but I am not going to correct him; if the numbers I have heard about Venice's galleys are accurate then we have got as many galleys as Venice and ours are rowed by well-fed archers with strong arms instead of sickly slaves.*

*On the other hand, our galleys are scattered all about earning coins and Venice's seem to be concentrated here waiting for the crusaders to begin moving.*

"Aye, and here come some of them. Coming up a little fast, are not they?" I asked Jeffrey. "I wonder where they are headed that is so important that they are willing to wear out their rowers to get there."

"Well, wherever it is I hope they have lookouts up on their masts to see us."

"Oh my God. Look."

What I was exclaiming about with such a shocked sound in my voice was the sharp turn the leading Venetian galley was suddenly making—instead of going past us within easy hailing distance it was turning towards us with fighting men on its deck. Its intentions were clearly hostile.

*What is going on here? This is impossible.*

"Ship oars. Battle stations to repel boarders. Ship oars, goddamn it," Jeffrey roared a few seconds before the Venetian came up alongside us and the sailors on its crowded deck began throwing grapples on to ours.

Out of the corner of my eye I could see another Venetian galley swerving towards us to come in on our other side. And there were several more coming up behind them.


****** *Samuel from Haywards Heath*

I am a lucky man and that is for sure. Sergeant Jeffrey sent me up here on the mast because I did not have a spare bowstring under my cap at the last inspection—and it is a damn good thing he did for I am truly happy not to be down in the middle of all that fighting on the deck.

I just wish I had me some kind of real weapon in case one them buggers tries to climb up here to get me. But I do not—me sword and shield are still under me seat and me damn bow and quivers are still hanging on the pegs.

I yelled down and warned them when all them galleys was still way off, did not I? But it did not do any good, did it? Old Jeffrey did not do a damn thing but keep right on rowing easy and they just pulled up on us slick as goose grease.

"Hey, down there on the deck. Watch out. There is another of the buggers coming up on the port side. Sergeant Jeffrey; sergeant, there are two more of the bastards coming up on the port side." *Christ, they cannot hear me for all the shouting and noise. Jesus, what if they have archers?—I am a sitting goose up here.*

It is something to see. Yes, it is and it is not my fault. I warned the sergeant; yes, I did, but they came right up on without us trying to do anything to stop them or get away until it was too late. They almost got some of our oars and would have done if the lads had not pulled them in quick-like.

I can see it all from up here. Our boys are coming up the stairs with their weapons and shields like their arses are on fire. They are shouting and screaming as they come up and the pirates or whoever they are being cut down and pushed back.

It is all chaos and confusion. I saw one of our men, I think it were Peter the smith from Chester, stumble and go down. Then someone I do not know seemed to go down on top of Peter when he reached down to help him to his feet.

I am all alone up here even though there are three pirate galleys lashed to one side of ours and two to the other side. The fighting is continuing to spread to the decks of all of them. Suddenly, I realise I am shouting encouragements and warnings to the men below who cannot hear me and some of our men are coming up the mast carrying bows and quivers.

I better move higher so they can use the lookout's nest to shoot as we have all practised. As I am climbing, I suddenly see a pirate with a bow on the deck of the farthest galley—it do not look like much of a bow, but he is aiming it up towards me and the men climbing up below me. Oh damn.

***** *Thomas*

The Venetians threw their grapples and swarmed aboard as our archers come charging up from the rowing decks with their small galley shields and swords. I pushed Cardinal Bertoli into the little deck castle up front and grabbed a shield and sword off the deck rack. So did everyone else on the deck except Jeffrey; he grabbed up one of the long pikes with blades and hooks.

For the first few seconds, we were pushed back and almost overwhelmed by a rush of the pirates—*they are Venetians, by God.* But then more and more and more of our archers reached the deck until it was so packed there was hardly room to push out a bow or swing a sword or pike.

Within an instant, some of our men began stepping over the railings on to our attackers' galleys to get out of the press and have more room to fight. It is not something we trained them to do. They were trained to fight and they are moving on to the Venetians' decks instinctively to get room to use their swords and draw their bows.

A sailor with a sword and wild eyes came at me making a wild slashing swing with his sword. His face registered surprise when I threw up my shield to block it and swept my single-edged blade down and across his stomach in a great slice—and felt it bite. He started screaming as I used my shield to push him back into the mass of Venetians behind him.

*They are sailors, by God. They do not know how to fight. We have got a chance.*

I was not the only one who realised the poor quality of the Venetians.

"They are not fighting men; they are just the dregs off the quays," I heard Jeffrey roar. "They are not fighting men at all. Kill them, lads. Yes, Harry, kill them all."

Slowly but surely the tide of the fighting turned in our favour as more and more of our archers reached the deck and the fighting increasingly spilled over on to the enemy galleys, which had lashed themselves to us and each other. All our hours of practise and training were paying off. We were taking casualties but nothing like they were.

I was standing next to the mast bellowing a very unpriestly "kill them, kill them" chant with all the other men, with my shield up and stabbing towards a man in front of me, when suddenly I was somehow knocked to the deck and everything got confused.

The next thing I remember is trying to struggle to my feet and being unable to do so because someone with a smashed in head and an arrow in his chest was sprawled out on top of me.

*I do not know how much time passed before I finally got pulled to my feet and realised one of our lookouts must have fallen from the mast and landed on me. By the time I got up, our deck was covered with dead and wounded men, mostly Venetians, and all the fighting was on the enemy galleys which lashed themselves to ours.*

"Come on, lads," I shouted to no one in particular as everything suddenly cleared in my head and I once again realised what was happening.

"Grab those pikes and follow me."

***** *Ralph from Liverpool*

When I heard the order to repel boarders, I grabbed my shield and sword from under my rowing seat, pulled my bow off the pegs where it was hanging, and rushed to the stairs just as we were trained and practised almost every day. It is the first time I have ever done it for real. It is very exciting for sure.

There was a crowd of men at the stairs and Gregory was just ahead of me as we pushed and jostled our way up on to the deck. Gregory's the chosen man in charge of Willy's squad. Willy sits on the bench in front of me next to the hull. He is my best mate. We are both from Liverpool, are not we?

Everyone was shouting and pushing. No one wanted to be the last man to reach the deck and make Sergeant Jeffrey unhappy. It always leads to extra duty bailing out the water in the sump and being the last to get a shore leave.

We spread out as we came off the stairs, and the noise on the slippery and tossing deck was the loudest I have ever heard what with all the screaming and shouting. It is a good thing we have to wear our tunics all the time or I would not know who I am supposed to go after.

Then it happened. The deck was bouncing up and down from the waves as I moved toward a man with a strange clothes and a white beard. He was carrying a sword and was obviously not one of us. But then in the confusion and pushing, I stepped on the leg of someone who's fallen down on the deck—whoever it was moved his leg as I stepped on it and as I tripped and fell there was a tremendous blow on my neck that knocked me all the way down.

Somehow I was on the deck at the very front of our galley beyond where the stairs come up from the rowing benches. I tried to get up but I could not move. All I could do was watch. For a few seconds, I could see the legs of the men moving around me and sometimes their faces as they shouted and screamed and used their shields and swords. But then they just faded away.

***** *Sergeant Captain Jeffrey*

Thomas was knocked to the deck next to me when our lookout man came down on top of him. I was too busy to help pull him back on his feet what with a swarthy sailor coming at me screaming in Italian and waving a sword about like he had never used one before.

I instinctively parried the sailor's rather tentative thrust with my shield and used my own sword to stick him straight in the belly.  Then I bashed him in his twisted face with my galley shield, gave a great pull to jerk my blade out, and concentrated on the man coming up behind him.

It turned out that I did not have to worry about the man coming at me.  He took one more step towards me and then one of our men off to his side knocked him out of the way with his shield and shoulder—and a split second later a great slashing pike blade came down from somewhere and split his head in two all the way down to his shoulders.

The deck was already slippery from blood and covered with bodies and struggling men when, a few seconds later, I grabbed up one of the pikes for myself and vaulted across the deck railing to get to the galley decks where fighting was still going on hot and heavy.

It was not long before the surviving Venetians began turning away from the fight and diving down below their decks where their terrified slaves were chained to the lower tier of rowing benches.

Some of our men had their blood up and followed them down.

"Do not kill them all, lads," I shouted several times. "We need to question them first."

I never thought about Thomas again until we finished mopping up the Venetians. Our archers were already trying to help our wounded men when I finally went looking for him amongst the heaps of dead and horribly wounded men on the deck. Then, to my great relief, I saw him coming out of the stern castle with Cardinal Bertoli.

***** *Sergeant Captain Jeffrey*

"They obviously followed us out of Venice and had it planned. But why did they do it?"

That was the question I asked Thomas when I finally find him standing with a bloody sword in front of the doorway to the little castle where he had shoved the Cardinal when the fighting started.

"I think I know but I am not sure," was Thomas's response.

We immediately threw the dead and seriously wounded Venetians over the side and only kept those who were not dying for questioning.

An hour later we had our answers and, of course, whilst we are questioning them and throwing them overboard, our men were doing everything they could to help those of our wounded men we might be able to save and giving a soldier's mercy to those we could not. Our casualties were surprising light under the circumstances. The Venetians, we discovered, were mostly sailors who had never been trained to fight and barely outnumbered us because all of their rowers were galley slaves.

Thomas and the Cardinal put on their robes and mitres and came out to bless the dead and dying Venetians—which was all of them since, after we finished questioning them, they were put over the side despite their desperate screams and pleas for mercy from those who are still alive. It is the fate of pirates.

Our own wounded were taken to the stern castle to be sewed up by the galley's sailmaker and given hefty helpings of flower paste for their pain; our men who had been killed were laid out in a row on the deck so they could be properly prayed at and blessed before we drop their bodies into the water. Several were so badly mangled it was hard to know who they were.

"Whose head is that up by the bow—ours or theirs?"

"That is Ralph's head, the poor sod. And that is the rest of him over there next to Willy the smith. They were good friends. Both being from Liverpool and all."

***** *Thomas*

We learnt two things from the Venetian survivors before they went over the side. The first is that the Venetians somehow found out about what is in the Pope's message to his representative and were trying to stop it from being delivered to the crusaders. The second thing is that there are relatively few actual fighting men on the Venetian galleys and they are not well trained to fight.

Almost all the Venetians we questioned were sailors who were used to their enemies surrendering when they swarmed aboard their galleys and cogs and began waving their swords about. To a man, the Venetians I questioned expressed their surprise at finding so many well-armed fighting men on our galley. They thought our galleys would be like theirs and those of the Moorish pirates—two or three dozen sailors who

# Chapter Twelve
*Surprise and betrayal.*

It was starting to get dark and the sea was getting choppy by the time Jeffrey finished appointing five small prize crews for the Venetian prizes. Their slaves were told they would be unchained and freed as soon as they reach Cyprus.

Whilst all that was happening, working parties of our sailors and archers were offloading most of our supplies to top up the supplies and water the prizes already have on board—so they can make it all the way to Cyprus without having to make port calls. At least, that is what we hope. A pouch of coins was given to each of the were barely trained to fight and a lot of chained slaves to do the rowing.

With five galleys and some additional soldiers from the city, they expected to outnumber us by five to one and for us to surrender and be killed without much of a fight. It never dawned on them, at least not until it was too late, that our rowers would all be fighting men and we would be better armed and better trained to fight than they were.

prize sergeants in case he had to stop along the way for supplies.

The only Venetian slaves who would not sail for Cyprus in chains were four overjoyed Englishmen. They were released immediately so they could come with us when we return to England.

In a few minutes we will cast off the last two prizes, put up the sail on our galley, and begin rowing into Pula with our wounded. We should be in Pula in the morning if the weather holds and our pilot is right about where we are positioned in relation to the port.

We are going to Pula because the Pope's legate is thought to be there trying to convince the city to pay Venice's taxes so the crusaders can use the tax coins to pay for their transportation to Egypt.

And we need to hurry because the Venetians and the crusaders obviously know of the Pope's order and will undoubtedly attempt to collect as much money as possible before the Christian cities find out about it, even if it means an attack. Once the Orthodox Christian cities learn of the Pope's order, the threat of a crusader attack if they do not pay will be gone and they will never be willing to pay.

\*\*\*\*\*

Cardinal Capua is almost certainly traveling on a Venetian galley. That no longer worries us because we now know the Venetians' poor fighting ability. What does worry me is that there are a lot more Venetians and, until the contents of the letter are known to the crusaders, they will continue to try to stop it from being delivered even if it means killing us all.

In any event, it was clear to me and Cardinal Bertoli that we need to reach Cardinal Capua as soon as possible—and we need to do it quickly before the Venetians find out that their initial effort to prevent the letter's delivery failed and they make another attempt.

There is no question about it—we will be in great danger from the Venetians until the Pope's letter is delivered and the crusaders know they cannot attack Christian cities to get the coins they need to pay the Venetians for their transportation to the Holy Land.

*****

We reached Pula's little harbour about three hours after the sun came up. The tents of the crusaders' large camp were clearly visible to the south of the city walls as we dropped our sail and rowed into the harbour. The village did not even have a proper quay, just a couple of short wooden wharves coming out from the beach in front of the city gate.

Cardinal Capua is undoubtedly at the local bishop's residence and so, with an idler from the wharf trotting alongside to guide us and four archers as guards, Cardinal Bertoli and I hurried there to deliver the Pope's letter to his legate— the sooner Cardinal Capua informs the crusaders they will be excommunicated if they attack a Christian city, the better. Then we can row for England.

We were hurrying because until the crusaders are informed of the Pope's threat, we would all be in great danger from the Venetians. They are obviously willing to kill even a cardinal to prevent the crusaders from learning about the Pope's message.

\*\*\*\*\*

Tomas of Perugia turned out to be the local bishop, and his residence was a fine stone house next to the church of Saint Mary Formosa. Cardinal Capua, the Pope's personal representative to the crusaders, was indeed staying with him and, as one might well imagine, they were absolutely astonished to see us and receive the Pope's letter.

They both read the Pope's letter and then listened whilst we told them about the attack of the Venetian galleys. The bishop's servants rushed to bring us bread, cheese, and breakfast wine whilst we talked. The two churchmen both immediately understood the significance of the Pope's parchment and why the Venetians were willing to go to such extreme lengths to stop the crusaders from finding out about it.

Bishop Tomas and the Pope's legate shared both good news and bad news with us as we ate. The good news was about Pula; it had already given in the crusader's demands for Venice's taxes without a fight. The bad news was about the much larger and more prosperous port of Zara to the south; it was not willing to pay and was about to be attacked. The Pope's letter had arrived just in time.

Cardinal Capua professed to be taken aback by the contents of the Pope's letter. He was, he said, concerned the crusaders would not believe the letter is from the Pope. He wanted us with him when he met with the crusader leadership to help convince them the letter really was from the Pope and the Pope was truly serious about his threat to excommunicate them.

We agreed, and he immediately sent one of Bishop Tomas's men to the crusader camp with a message asking its leaders to drop whatever they are doing and hurry to the bishop's private room in the church of Saint Mary Formosa on a matter of great importance.

*****

Cardinal Bertoli and I met with the crusader leadership several hours later in Bishop Tomas's little office, which opens into the church near the altar. Surprisingly, the Bishop was there but Cardinal Capua was not. According to Bishop Tomas, the Cardinal had been called away on urgent business related to the crusade. He will be represented by a priest from his staff, Father Antonio.

Also surprisingly, only two crusaders, Robert Thibaut of Champagne and Henri of St.

Dizier, came to the meeting. Both are French knights and both were armed and wearing armour. The door was quickly barred by Father Antonio "so we can talk privately," and I immediately got the feeling something was seriously wrong. The hair on the back of my neck was literally standing on end.

The six of us did not even have a chance to sit down at the Bishop's table before Cardinal Capua's priest revealed just how wrong things had gone.

"You two are quite foolish, you know," Father Antonio said. "And now it is going to be the death of you both."

"What are you saying, Father Antonio?" demanded the usually cheerful and ever optimistic Cardinal Bertoli with more than a little surprise in his voice.

Father Antonio's reply surprised us.

"Do you really think we were not warned about the letter you are carrying from the Pope and that we are going to tell our crusaders to call off the crusade and go home because of it?"

"The Pope is not ordering you to end your crusade," Cardinal Bertoli responded with a touch of astonishment in his voice. "He is only telling you not to attack innocent Christians in order to get the money needed to pay for your transportation to Acre. In the name of God, Antonio, it is the Pope who called for the crusade. He has not changed his mind about the crusade; he does not want it stopped. His letter does not stop it."

"Yes, it does," the priest replied rather forcefully, "because without the coins the cities owe Venice, we cannot get the crusaders to

Jerusalem. Thanks to Venice we finally have a way to get the coins and we are not going to give them up—Jerusalem is much more important than a cardinal and few small ports on the Adriatic."

"The crusaders here and in Venice are good men," Cardinal Bertoli replied indignantly. "I know many of them. They will never attack Zara if the Pope tells them not to do so."

*Bertoli is seriously naïve, but this is not the time to explain the crusaders to him.*

"Unfortunately, you are right, of course," Father Antonio agreed. "The crusaders would not attack Zara or even threaten it if the Pope says they should not—that is why we cannot allow you to tell them about the Pope's letter."

I stepped closer to the two knights and pleaded with them most abjectly.

"Good knights, brave men. Surely, you would not harm high officials of the Church in order to keep the Pope's letter a secret."

The amused sneers on of the faces of the two knights told the Bishop and me all we needed to know. They certainly would and that is what they intend to do. There was no doubt about it.

"And you, Bishop Tomas?" I asked with a quaver in my voice as I turned towards Bishop Tomas and backed even closer to the knights whilst I waved my hands about in despair. I was so overwhelmed and distraught I was almost staggering.

"Are you to be killed with us or have you joined with these three who would defy the Pope and murder us to keep his letter from the crusaders?"

"Bishop Tomas is with us," the priest answered for him with a sneer. "And with his share of the coins and treasure from here and Zara he will be a cardinal in Rome for certain. Perhaps he will even take Cardinal Bertoli's place after Cardinal Bertoli disappears."

The priest smiled and nodded to Bishop Tomas who nodded back his agreement and returned his smile.

"Perhaps it is God's will that Cardinal Bertoli and I should die here."

I said the words with pleading resignation in my voice as I lifted my arms in supplication towards the knights and heaven—and the arms of my robe slide back and my wrist knives came out.

My move to bring out my double-bladed wrist knives caught the crusader knights totally by surprise—as it should since they would not expect it from a bishop, and William and I have practised doing it almost every day for twenty years.

The two crusaders did not even have time to blink before I jammed the knife in my right hand deep into Count Thibaut's eye and thrust the one in my left straight through Sir Henri's greying beard and into his throat.

Count Thibaut instinctively jerked back as I pushed the knife into his eye, so I make a fast step towards him and jammed it in all the way in with a hard push. I could feel it jar my wrist as the point hit the bone in the back of his skull and stuck.

He dropped straight down and his legs began shaking and trembling. That was a good sign, of course, his legs trembling that is. It meant he was a goner and would be no more trouble. Unfortunately, he was a large man and took my blade down with him.

Sir Henri, in contrast, just stood there with his hands clutching his throat and looking at me with disbelief in his eyes—until I pulled out my knife with a sideways pull that sliced his throat even more. Despite his great wound, Sir Henri stepped forward and desperately tried to grab at me.

I quickly stepped back with the bloody knife in my hand and watched as he staggered to the Bishop's table and held his neck with one hand whilst using his other hand to hold himself up. All the time he was staring at me in disbelief as great surges of blood pumped out over his hand.

***** *Thomas*

Time seemed to stand still, and no one moved or said a word until Sir Henri sank to his knees on the floor.  Then both the Bishop and the priest ran for the barred door.  They did not make it.

Cardinal Capua's priest went first.  Father Antonio screamed a high-pitched scream as I shoved my knife deep into his liver and ripped it upward with both hands as he fumbled with the bar holding the door closed.

Then I pulled it out and knocked him to the ground with my elbow and went after dear old Bishop Tomas—but only after I stomped on the priest's neck so hard I could feel the bones break.  *I was not always employed as a priest, was I?*

"Please, no.  Please.  I did not mean it.  For the love of God, I am innocent.  Please, do not.  No.  Help.  Murder.  Help.  Please, do not kill me.  I will tell you everything.  I will pay you.  I will—"

For a few, brief seconds I had to chase the Bishop around the table and listen to him babble his screams for help.  But I soon caught him.  He flailed wildly about and even tried to scratch me in the face as I grabbed him by the front of his robe with my left hand and pulled him to me.

"You've already told us everything we need to know about you—you are a murderer and a false priest."

That was what I said in a snarling whisper as I held the Bishop firmly by his robe and slowly pushed my knife into his stomach and up into his heart—and twisted it as he arched his back and sucked in his stomach in a futile effort to get off it whilst he screamed.

It was a strange scream. For a few seconds, Bishop Tomas gave a high-pitched squeal like pigs squeal when they are being slaughtered—but then it stopped as he sank to his knees on the dirt floor and began sobbing and trying to talk and whimper and beg and scream all at the same time. I held him for a minute or two until he stopped making noise and faded away.

There was a lot of shouting and furious pounding on the door when I finally let loose of the Bishop's robe and give him a little push so he fell to the floor in a rapidly widening pool of blood. His feet began their death trembles and he began to piss and shite as I leaned over to pull my knife out, wiped it on my robe, and put it back into the leather holder on my left wrist.

Finally, I turned my attention to Cardinal Bertoli.

"Are you all right, Cardinal?"

That was what I asked a white-faced and trembling Cardinal Bertoli as I tried to pull my other knife out of Sir Robert's eye. It was firmly stuck. Finally, I put my foot on his head and used both hands to pull my knife out with a great tug and a grunt.

Cardinal Bertoli did not answer my question. He could not talk; he was leaning against the wall and looking at me; it looked like he was about to have a great seizure and fall down. It happens when a man's blood gets too warm.

## Chapter Thirteen

*The hurried departure.*

We waited to open the door to our archers and the Bishop's servants until Cardinal Bertoli recovered his voice and everyone had finished their dying and taken their final piss and shite— and my own heart had slowed from beating so fast I thought I might burst myself. Whilst we waited for our would-be murderers to finish their dying, I told Cardinal Bertoli the story we would tell to explain what happened. He never said a word, just stood there with his mouth hanging open and nodded as I spoke.

*People who die always seem to piss and shite at the end. Some priests say it is so their bodies will be clean as possible when they meet God and are judged. But I wonder if it is possible that it something else, since even the greatest of sinners like these four seem to do it.*

There was a great and growing crowd of anxious and shouting clerics and archers in the church when I finally unbarred the door between the Bishop's private room and the church. Then, without letting the rapidly growing crowd in, Cardinal Bertoli and I stood in the entrance to the Bishop's room and I briefly explained in Latin and French the sad details of what had happened.

Cardinal Bertoli stood next to me and made speechless nods of agreement and crossed himself after each point I made.

*The floor was everywhere sticky and muddy from all the blood, and the little room smelled terrible as battlefields always do. We have got to clear these people out of the church and get some archers here from the galley before someone shows up with weapons and thinks to question us closely. It is really foul in here and I feel a bit like I am going to be sick. It is a good thing I have not eaten for some time.*

"These two knights had a great fight about how to spend money donated by Pula and killed the good Bishop and this fine priest when they tried to stop the fighting as good priests should. Is not that so, Cardinal Bertoli?" He did not answer; just nodded.

Then I explained what will probably happen next.

"Such good Christian martyrs these two churchmen are for trying to stop the fighting and bloodshed. Fortunately, the Cardinal and I were able to give them the necessary last rites before they died so they are now safely in heaven.

"We will, of course, be leaving immediately to take their bodies back to Rome for a proper burial. When the Pope hears about their saintly behaviour, he will undoubtedly want to canonise them."

*Cardinal Bertoli and I agreed on the 'necessary last rites' they are to receive—we are going to dump the treacherous bastards in the sea so they would not be able to foul a cemetery holding decent people. Well, Bertoli did not actually agree; he sort of just stood there and did not argue when I told him what we are going to do and why.*

*****

The real leaders of the crusaders showed up soon after we sent a couple of the Bishop's ashen-faced priests running to fetch them. Seven crusaders came to meet with us to "get an important message from Pope Innocent." They were led by two Frenchmen who introduced themselves as Boniface of Montferrat and Simon de Montfort.

We closed the door to the scene in the Bishop's office, shooed the archers and onlookers from the church, and stood with the crusaders in a circle in front of the altar of the church. Then I repeated our story about the fight and read the Pope's letter to them. To a man, they were shocked and appalled about the tragedy of the deaths and the contents of the Pope's letter.

*The crusaders believe the men died fighting each other because for them there was no other possible explanation—they could not conceive of a middle-aged English bishop and an elderly cardinal killing all four of the men even though my robe was soaked with blood.*

The crusaders did not actually read the Pope's letter, of course, since they cannot read. Rather Cardinal Bertoli read it to them in Latin—which they do not speak. I added my nod of agreement at the appropriate places.

As the good cardinal read the Pope's letter to them in Latin, I simultaneously translated what he was reading into French—with a few embellishments of my own which Cardinal Bertoli did not catch because he only speaks Italian and Latin. It was an altogether satisfactory process.

There were nine of us in all and we talked at length until what was to be done next was agreed by everyone. It took well over an hour to work out the details and come up with an agreeable plan of action.

What we agreed is that Montfort and Montferrat will immediately go to the crusader camp and inform the men about the Pope's letter. Then, as soon as they finish explaining things to their men, de Montfort will return and sail with us to Venice so he and Cardinal Bertoli can explain the Pope's letter to the crusaders who are still there. The crusaders who are here in Pula will remain here under the command of Montferrat until a decision is reached as to what they are to do next.

*Nobody mentioned the coins the crusaders recently took from Pula and I forgot to inquire*

*about them. It really does not matter. Besides,*
*the crusaders will need them to buy food whilst*
*they are here and passage back to Venice or*
*wherever it is they decide to go next.*

It was quickly clear by his responses that
Montfort is a particularly pious man and a true
believer in the special relationship the Pope is
said to have with God. He was quite intense,
almost emotional, when he told us he will
explain to the crusaders that what happened to
Thibaut of Champagne and Henri of St. Dizier is
what a crusader must expect if he disobeys the
Pope and the Will of God—God will intervene
and punish him.

\*\*\*\*\*

As soon as the crusaders leave the church
to inform their men, Cardinal Bertoli and I intend
to go straight to Jeffrey's galley with its archers

escorting us in case there is more trouble. We will be similarly careful when we go ashore to meet the crusaders in Venice—neither we nor any member of Jeffrey's crew will go ashore when we drop off Cardinal Bertoli and de Montfort to meet with the crusaders who are still there.

*There is no sense giving the Venetians or anyone else a chance to organise yet another surprise attack—or not to be ready if one comes. I had sent an archer to get reinforcements and Jeffrey himself had led almost the entire company of out-of-breath archers in a run for the church. They were still catching their breaths when the crusaders arrived.*

As you might imagine, Cardinal Bertoli and I are not going to meet with any of the crusaders unless de Montfort and his men and a strong guard of archers are present, or meet with any Venetians anywhere for that matter. There is much too much potential danger if the friends of the two French knights find out what really happened and decide to seek revenge. The same for the Venetians who might have had a family member or friend on the galleys that attacked us—the truth about what happened is almost certain to get out sooner or later because so many of our archers and sailors were involved.

*****

Cardinal Bertoli and I walked out of the Bishop's room and headed for our galley as soon as the seven crusaders hurried out of the church to carry word of the Pope's letter to the crusader camp. We will take the two dead churchmen with us as we would be expected to do if they are potential saints and wait on the galley for de

Montfort. We will sail for Venice as soon as he arrives. De Montfort said we can expect him and a dozen or so of his retainers before sundown.

There were curious crowds in the streets of Pula as Cardinal Bertoli and I walked from the church to the quay in the afternoon sun with our substantially reinforced guard of archers. People were unusually quiet and stared at us intently and made the sign of the cross as we went past them with Jeffrey's archers surrounding us and the hastily commandeered push cart carrying the two dead churchmen and pulled by the church's priests.

The people standing along the cobblestoned street know something significant has happened but they do not know what it is and are afraid to ask. The priests, on the other hand, had heard my explanation. To my surprise, they insisted on pulling the cart containing the "saints'" earthly remains and actually argued with each other as to who should have the honour.

The behaviour of the priests surprised me so much that I asked Cardinal Bertoli about it as we walked back to the galley. He said it was undoubtedly because they hoped to be summoned to Rome to participate in the "saints'" beatification.

"They are going to be sorely disappointed," I said with determination in my voice.

"I would not be too sure about that if we stick to the story that they are martyrs," was Cardinal Bertoli's reply. "Miracles often occur after prayers and Bishop Tomas comes from an extremely devout family, which may well be rich enough to discover some."

"Well, there sure as hell would not be any relics so people remember them; those two murderers are for the fish and that is for damn sure," I said.

*****

De Montfort was as good as his word. He arrived with his men before the sun goes down. There were thirteen of them in all including himself.

Until we reach Venice, de Montfort will be bedded in with Cardinal Bertoli, Peter, Jeffrey, and me in the little deck castle at the front of the galley; his men will be in the bigger deck castle at the rear of the galley, which usually shelters the galley's sergeants. The galley's unhappy sergeants will temporarily join our archers and sailors who, as usual, will sleep rough on and around the rowing benches and use their long, hooded sheepskins to keep themselves warm and dry.

It was growing dark when our galley's rowing drum finally started and we began making our way out of the harbour bound for Venice. It had been a long day and I was suddenly very tired—but not too tired to give one final order as I headed off with Cardinal Bertoli for some much needed rest.

"Throw the garbage overboard in the middle of the night," I told Jeffrey with a jerk of my thumb towards the bodies of the two churchmen who tried to kill us.

"No. Wait. We cannot do that," Bertoli objected. "I have been thinking. We must treat them as potential saints until the Holy Father decides what story he wants us to tell about what happened here. He may not want anyone to know the priests and crusaders defied him and died; or he may want it known. We can only pray he and those around him will want it known—otherwise, we might be silenced to make sure the secret is kept."

"You cannot be serious? Do you really think the Pope or some of the men around him might try to silence us?"

"Of course, I am serious; the Church is always looking for saints to inspire people and powerful families always want to have a saint in their family—we are the only ones who know they are not."

I could not think of anything to say. *I have been a fool. I should have thought up a better explanation.*

## Chapter Fourteen

*Preparing to sail.*

Venice came in sight late the next afternoon. The sky was overcast, and we did not know what kind of reception to expect—so we slowly rowed into the crowded harbour on high alert and ready to instantly fight or run.

Bales of arrows had been brought out of the cargo hold and stacked up all over the deck; four archers with good 'long' eyes were up in our expanded lookout's nest; sergeants inspected every man's weapons; and Jeffrey and his sergeants spent time in every corner of the galley making sure every man knew what he was to do under the various circumstances. Hopefully, of course, our preparations will not be needed.

We did not tie up at the quay when we bumped up against it. Instead, some of Jeffrey's sailors used the hooks on our pikes to hold the galley against the quay whilst de Montfort and his men and climbed up to it. We boosted Cardinal Bertoli up to join them and then backed off about forty feet from the quay. We will wait out here in the harbour for them to return.

The Cardinal is going with de Montfort to meet with the crusaders and any Venetian officials who want to talk about the payments that must be paid if Venetian galleys and cogs are to carry the crusaders to Egypt and the Holy Land. I am not going with them and neither are any of our men.

I hope Cardinal Bertoli will be safe. Whilst we were sailing here he and I talked about things at length when de Montfort was not around. Should he or should he not be accompanied by a guard of our archers? Should Peter go with him so he would have an assistant and a messenger?

After much discussion and prayer, the Cardinal finally decided to not avail himself of my offer to provide him with archers as guards or, at least, Peter or a reliable archer sergeant as an assistant. He thinks he will be safe so long as he is with de Montfort and his men.

He was probably right but then again that was what we thought at Pula when we went ashore to look for Cardinal Capua at the bishop's residence next to the church. I reminded Bertoli of this to no avail—he decided that being with de

Montfort would be more than enough to protect his safety.

The Cardinal promised he would lie if he was asked about the Venetian galleys and say he spent the entire voyage so sea poxed in the little castle that he would not have known if the world had come to an end as some monks have recently been predicting. For my part, I agreed I had play dumb myself for the next few days even though the fate of the Venetian galleys is sure to come out sooner or later.

"God and the Pope will forgive us for our lies," we both agreed.

*I wonder if our prizes have reached Cyprus?*

*****

Somewhere along the line during his visit with the crusaders, Cardinal Bertoli will decide whether to stay longer in Venice with the crusaders or sail with us back to Rome to report to the Pope. He will stay, he confided to me, if it appears the crusaders might still flout the Pope's orders. Either way, he is to return to the galley in the morning no later than three hours after sunup.

If he decides to stay in Venice, he will come tell us in person. If we do not see him in person by three hours after sunup, we will immediately leave without him and report to the Pope that the Venetians and crusaders have captured or killed him—and we further agreed that any message purporting to be from him and asking us to wait longer will be false and mean we are in danger of being attacked again by the Venetians and should immediately leave.

We were not taking chances. As soon as Cardinal Bertoli and the crusaders disembark, we moved a little ways away from the quay and took a position with our bow pointing towards the harbour entrance and our oars in the water. From here we can also quickly return to the quay if necessary.

It is a good thing we did not stay at the quay. A hostile crowd began gathering on the quay almost immediately. Somehow word had reached Venice that the five Venetian galleys have been lost and we might be responsible.

*Wait till they hear about the Pope's letter and find out that the crusaders will not be able to pay them.*

Sure enough. Some Venetian officials arrive and shout out to us from the quay. They want us to come ashore so they can talk to us.

We waved our hands to acknowledge their request, nodded our heads in agreement, and stayed on board. *I may be stupid but I am not that stupid.*

Several merchants also shouted out to us. Jeffrey recognised them as men he is dealt with previously for supplies. They wanted to know if we would like to buy any supplies. They have, they told us, just received some particularly tender young sheep. Their inquiry is normal and it was quite encouraging that they made it openly in front of the crowd—*Venice is a city of merchants and money comes before everything else around here every time.*

Several of the merchants had themselves rowed out to us in a dinghy and we ordered flour, firewood, water, one hundred chickens, and twenty live sheep to be delivered first thing in the morning via small boats and lighters.

Whilst we were negotiating with the merchants, the Venetian officials who had hailed us earlier were joined by several others. The new arrivals arrived with a force of guards carrying swords and shields, huddled with the men who initially hailed us, and then hailed us themselves.

The new arrivals seem to be senior to the first batch. They acted quite full of themselves and began to shout out very specific orders— they wanted us to come ashore so they could talk to us about the missing galleys.

"Pigs will fly before I will go back to the quay except with a dinghy to pick up the Cardinal."

Jeffrey said it quietly to me out of the side of his mouth as we stood side by side smiling and nodding our agreement to the officials on the quay and lifting our hands to acknowledge our acceptance of their order.

"I wonder how they found out?" was my response.

Jeffrey said, "Maybe one of our prizes was retaken or had to put in somewhere for repairs or supplies whilst we were in Pula. Who knows? What matters is they think we are responsible for their missing galleys—which, of course, we are—and what particularly matters is what they intend to do about it."

Then, after a pause, Jeffrey added another thought.

"Or maybe all they know is that their galleys were supposed to intercept us—and now they have all disappeared and we are here even though the weather's been good. It does not take much of a carpenter to put those two facts together."

"Well, they are seriously pissed about their missing galleys and that is a fact," was my reply as I gestured toward the growing crowd of Venetians standing on the quay and the rock throwers who periodically attempted to reach us.

Then I turned to Jeffrey and added a bit more with a wry smile and a joking tone to my voice.

"And if you think they are pissed now, just wait until they find out what is in the Pope's letter and discover the crusaders would not be able to pay them."

*****

What we were mostly doing whilst we waited for the Cardinal to return was staying just out of rock-throwing range, letting our men eat and rest to regain their strength, and watching the growing and increasingly noisy and threatening crowd.

A few rocks were thrown by enthusiastic young men, but we were too far off the quay so they splashed harmlessly into the water. Jeffrey, however, was ready for anything—our galley's deck was crowded with archers with their longbows by their sides amidst open bales of arrows. Most of them were napping in the morning sun.

Almost everyone not on the deck was sitting or napping on a rowing bench with his weapons near at hand—ready to row or fight as his sergeants ordered. The only exceptions were the men who periodically hung their dingles and arses out over the rear of the galley to piss or shite into the harbour. They inevitably waved to acknowledge the jeers and what were obviously ribald shouts from the nearby crowd.

The only thing certain is that we will not be sending any of our wounded men ashore for barbering or letting the Venetians know we have wounded men on board.

*****

We stayed on alert all that day and the night that followed. Nothing happened and there was no word from Cardinal Bertoli. The mob that had spent the previous afternoon jeering and shouting and throwing stones at us was long gone and our men fully rested by the time the sun finished circling the earth and came up the next morning.

Sunrise was unbelievably serene and peaceful. We could hear church bells in the city and everything was rather quiet except for squawking seagulls and a few men walking about on the quay. Jeffrey, Peter, and I were breaking our night of fasting by munching on some of the hot bread one of the cooks just handed us—and sipping bowls of the ale that somehow came aboard before our sudden departure from Pula.

In a few minutes, lighters and small boats will arrive and we will start taking on the supplies and water we ordered yesterday from the merchants who hailed us. Whilst we waited, we amused ourselves by watching the efforts of a big two-masted cog as its captain tried to work it into the mooring space we had hurriedly vacated yesterday when the mob arrived.

The cog came into the harbour under tow at daybreak and anchored off the quay just south of where we spent the night waiting for word from Cardinal Bertoli.

"Can you pull forward so the cog can come in and tie up?" was the hail in Italian from one of the workers on the quay.

I translated the request. It was eminently reasonable under the circumstances. It was not surprising when Jeffrey nodded and lifted his hand to signal agreement. A few minutes later our galley hoisted our two anchors, rowed a bit further out and towards the north, and re-dropped them.

"That should give them enough room," Jeffrey muttered to no one in particular. Almost immediately after we re-anchored in the new location, two lighters appeared our port side and threw lines up to our sailors. They were the first of the half dozen or so we were expecting to arrive and begin delivering the water and supplies we ordered from the merchants yesterday.

A few minutes later we were surrounded by lighters and the workmen on them were handing up bleating sheep and strings of squawking chickens with their legs tied together. Others were filling wooden buckets from a big tub in the middle of a lighter and handing them up to our men to pour the water into our own skins and barrels.

I was standing on the deck watching whilst I munched on a flatbread and a piece of cheese when Jeffrey walked back from supervising the unloading of the lighters. We stood together on our galley's deck for a moment without speaking and watched the two-masted cog trying to move into the quay and moor. Jeffrey was relaxed. He had finished making sure his sergeants know where he wants the supplies stacked and stored and there really was not much else for him to do except watch until the lighters finish making their deliveries.

Our men were similarly relaxed and eating flatbread which the cooks were busy frying and cutting pieces off a big cheese the cook had set out. It was altogether a nice morning before the heat of the day arrived. Yesterday's crowd and officials were nowhere to be seen.

The captain of the cog attempting to moor at the quay was obviously in a hurry. As soon as we agreed to move out of the way, a couple of small boats were launched from his cog to tow it to the quay.

We were already attached to the lighters and loading supplies by the time the cog got close enough for the sailors in the small boats to throw mooring lines to the quay so the workers on the quay could pull the cog in against it and moor it firmly in its place.

That was the cog's plan and it worked, but only partially.

Mooring lines were thrown to the quay and a gang of workers began to haul in the cog. They got its bow to the quay and successfully moored. But somehow the line attached to the stern of the cog got fouled or loose. It happened before the workers could finish pulling the stern of the cog up against the quay and mooring it into place— and just as the wind changed direction and picked up.

Jeffrey and I and Jeffrey's crew watched and listened in utter fascination as the stern of the cog slowly and inexorably floated further and further out from the quay and began swinging in a big circle around the cog's bow, which was still moored to the quay.

The loss of the mooring line would not have been too much of a problem except there was another even larger transport taking on cargo in the next space in front of the one trying to reach the quay. There was no question about the immediate problem—if the stern of the arriving cog was blown all the way around it was almost certainly going to hit the stern of the three-masted ship loading cargo in the next mooring space.

There was immediately much alarmed shouting and commotion aboard both the cog attempting to moor and the three-masted ship loading cargo in the next mooring space. A new mooring line was obviously in the process of being attached to the stern of the cog attempting to moor.

We watched with interest and a bit of amusement as a couple of sailors hauled the new line to the stern of the cog and secured it. Their intention was to then throw the new line to the workers waiting on the quay who would then haul the cog's stern to the quay.

Too late. It had taken the cog's sailors too long to get the new line ready and thrown to the workers on shore—the stern of the cog had already swung so far around that pulling on the new line would now cause the stern to hit the loading cargo transport in the next mooring space even harder.

There was much excitement and shouting on both the cog and the ship. Sailors with poles gathered along the railings of both transports to hold them apart whilst others raced to put wicker bales of old rags in place for use as bumpers to keep the two hulls apart.

It was almost amusing, and a crowd of idlers on our deck were watching and pointing at the frenzied activity and talking to each other and laughing about it. Even the men who were busy shifting the supplies from the lighters were watching and smiling and making comments about the cog's situation as they worked.

It stopped being amusing when someone on the cog attempted to stop the impending collision by casting off the line attaching the cog's bow to the quay. The entire two-masted transport was suddenly free to drift away from the quay. It could now be pushed away from the ship loading cargo in the next mooring berth and drift out into the harbour.

It worked.  The sailors aboard the transports were able to hold them apart so the cog could safely drift past the ship loading cargo—and straight towards where we were anchored just off the quay with flat-bottomed supply lighters attached to us and busy offloading their water and supplies.

"Cast off the lighters' lines.  Cast off the lighters' lines.  Hoist the anchors.  All rowers to their oars," Jeffrey boomed.  He was highly aggravated from the sound of his voice and rightly so as the drifting cog bore down on us.

Our men went from laughing and pointing to gasping in surprise and dismay.

Everywhere our men dropped whatever it is they were doing and dashed to their places as their sergeants began to shout and swear.  No one was more surprised than the merchants' men working on the small, flat-bottomed supply lighters provisioning us. They suddenly saw our galley cast off their lines and hoist its anchors and row off—leaving them dead in the water as an out of control two-masted cog was blown towards them by the wind.

All I could do is grasp the deck railing and watch as the slowly moving but totally out of control cog was blown into one of the lighters carrying our supplies and then into two others.

The merchants' men on the lighters were able to hold on but we watched in dismay as some of our supplies, including a pen of sheep and some flour barrels, slid off into the water when the hull of the slowly moving, runaway cog pushed against the lighter and tipped one side of it up so steeply that water began to come in over its lowered other side.

It was a near miss for us. Jeffrey had gotten us detached from the lighters and we rowed away from the drifting cog and the heads of the sheep swimming in the water just in time.

Jeffrey's unhappiness with the situation was evident in the curses he hurled at the crew of the runaway cog as it drifted past us pushing one of our lighters in front of it. Now we would have to row through the harbour in a great circle to get back to the lighters and what is left, if anything, of our water and supplies.

Jeffrey was furious and cursing—he could bring us back around to the lighters and the men clinging to them but he had no idea how we would ever hoist the swimming sheep on board.

"And if we do get them aboard, they will be so foul from being in the harbour water that they will probably sicken and die before we can eat them," he fumed.

We were barely and slowly underway to make our great circle and return to the lighters when one of the lookouts on the mast shouted down to report a small boat rowing hard in an effort to catch up with us.

Jeffrey stopped the rowing so it could come alongside. It did and a few minutes later the man in the dinghy handed up a parchment for "Signor la Bishop."

# Chapter Fifteen

*Our great surprise.*

The message the dinghy delivered was from Cardinal Bertoli. He would be delayed and he regretted having to ask us to delay our sailing until tomorrow morning. Uh oh; it was the signal for big trouble and for us to run for it. It was time for us to go and go fast.

"Jeffrey," I roared after I quickly read through the parchment a second time to make sure I had read it correctly. "It is a message from the Cardinal. He is delayed and wants us to wait and sail tomorrow."

Jeffrey understood immediately and began shouting new orders to his men. Less than a minute later the rowing drum began its rhythmic beat and we began picking our way through the densely packed shipping in the harbour leaving most of our food and water behind.

\*\*\*\*\*

Venice has a huge harbour so it was not until almost twenty minutes later that we reached the harbour entrance—and saw a huge fleet of Venetian war galleys waiting ahead of us. Most of them are galleys like ours with two banks of oars but there were even some of the older, Roman-style galleys with three. *My God! I was surprised and stunned. Where did they all come from?*

"My God, Jeffrey!  Where did they all come from?  Surely, they are not all out there waiting for us?"

Jeffrey did not even have time to answer my question before the Venetians answered it for him.  The closest galleys, the ones who could see us as soon as we could see them, began rowing—and they were rowing hard and straight at us.

"All hands to the oars except the lookouts," Jeffrey shouts after an instant's hesitation.  "Stand by to lower the sail.  Lower the sail."

*****

Jeffrey instantly ordered our port oars to pull forward and the starboard oars to pull backward.  In a matter of seconds our galley spun around and was pointed back into the crowded harbour with its sail down—and the closest of the fast closing Venetians looked to be less than a couple of thousand paces away.

"Maximum speed, Row Master, maximum speed."

We picked up more and more speed as more and more of our archers and sailors reached their rowing benches and the drummer's beat picked up to about as fast as I have ever heard it. Some of our oars had two men on them but most only had one due to the absence of the prize crews and the casualties we suffered in the battle with the Venetian galleys. On the other hand, almost all the rowers were archers—and they have stronger arms and shoulders than most men as a result of practising every day with their longbows and rowing.

"There is another entrance on the other side of the harbour. I am going to go back through the harbour and try to get us out through the other entrance."

Jeffrey was so excited he shouted his decision at me even though I was standing right next to him.

"Quick, follow me," he shouted over his shoulder as he dashed to the rear of the galley so he could stand on the roof of the stern deck castle. From there he could at the same time both look ahead at everything anchored in the harbour ahead of us and look down to see and talk to the rowing sergeant, the drummer, and the two rudder men.

I ran after Jeffrey and climbed up the three wooden steps to the stern castle's roof right behind him. So did his sailor sergeant and the sailor with a big voice who seemed to stay with him at all times to run his errands and shout his orders.

*The ability of a galley's captain to see what is directly in front of it is not quite as good if he stands on the roof of the deck castle in its stern instead of its bow but it is good enough, and it lets him give his rowing and steering orders directly to the galley's rowing sergeant and its rudder men. The castle roof is such a common place for galley captains to stand that there are even three wooden steps from the deck to the castle roof and a railing around it for him to hold.*

\*\*\*\*\*

We went back into the big harbour a whole lot faster than we had come out a few minutes earlier. Our galley picked up speed rapidly after we spun around and started back into the harbour, and it is a good thing we did—the Venetian galleys closed in rapidly on us whilst we were turning; the closest of them was less than five hundred paces behind us as we passed back through the harbour entrance and headed towards the crowd of masts in the harbour.

This was no time for me to tell Jeffrey how to captain his galley, but I did make a suggestion in the form of a question.

"Do you think the archers in the lookout nest can reach the lookouts and the rudder men and captains behind us?"

Jeffrey seized on the idea, quickly gave the order, and a few seconds later arrows began flying back towards our pursuers and two more of our very best archers were on their way up the mast to join the two already there.

A moment later, another order from Jeffrey sent a couple of nimble sailors to get arrows from the open bales which had been open on the deck ever since we sailed into the harbour yesterday. He ordered them to keep the archers on the mast nicely supplied. He also named off various archers who were to drop their oars and come on deck with their bows to join the shooting. They were, I was rather sure, his best men.

*****

Our rapidly moving galley plunged towards the mass of cargo transports anchored in the harbour as our arrows began to fly at the pursuers coming up behind us.

I jumped down from the roof, reached across a startled rower to grab his bow and quiver, and then waited anxiously whilst he found his wrist guard and handed it to me without missing a beat as he rowed a stroke with one arm. Then I bounded back up the stairs and began to push out arrows myself whenever I thought I saw someone within my range who would be more useful if they were dead or discouraged. *I was not always a priest.*

Suddenly, a thought flooded into my mind. The rudder men—I remembered what William and Harold had said about their fight with the Tunisian galleys that pursued them out of the Tunis harbour.

"Forget the men on the deck," I shouted at the archers. "Drop your arrows on their captain and rudder men whenever possible."

"Yes," shouted Jeffrey in agreement as he let loose another of his own shafts and turned to his loud-voiced talker. "Pass the word for the archers to ignore the men on deck and aim at the rudder men and captain and the lookouts. And tell Francis and Guy to open up more arrow bales."

Without a word being spoken, Jeffrey's sailor sergeant had taken over captaining the galley as Jeffrey and I joined in the shooting. We lurched this way and that as Stanley the mouth shouted the sailing sergeant's orders down to our rudder men and rowers.

The shouted orders to turn this way and that were almost continuous as we threaded our way through the cogs and ships anchored in the harbour. Once a sharp, shaking jolt ran through the galley and there was a shudder and a sharp cracking noise as we ran over something, probably a dinghy.

A few seconds later the sailing sergeant suddenly shouted with alarm in his voice.

"In oars.  In oars."

Our rowing drum suddenly stopped and we glided silently forward.  A few seconds later, there was a loud, banging crash and long scraping sound.  Some of the men and I were thrown off our feet.  When I scrambled to my feet, I could see we were scraping the side of some kind of cargo transport.  We were going by it so close I could have reached out and touched its hull.

Then I heard, "Out oars and row, lads, row.  Out oars.  Put your backs into it."

When I got back on my feet, I could see our lead pursuer.  It was a galley much like ours with two tiers of rowers.  It had almost caught up to us when we stopped rowing and scraped against the anchored cog. It was not more than a couple of hundred paces behind us.

Just as I was about loose another arrow, our pursuer suddenly wobbled and then turned straight into the anchored cog it was passing with a loud crash and a crunching sound that rolled over the harbour water behind us.

The archers on our deck gave a great cheer and we all temporarily stopped shooting arrows for lack of a target. Someone must have gotten a rudder man.

*Good. I need a rest. My arms are getting tired.*

*****

Our lack of targets did not last long. We came past an anchored cargo cog just as a Venetian galley came past it on the other side.

How it was we never even saw the Venetian until it reached us totally escaped me, but here it is.

We were running side by side through the packed harbour and the Venetian's deck was crowded with shouting men. Their galley was so close and the men on its deck so densely packed that the longbows of our archers could hardly miss.

I spotted a man who appears to be giving orders and sent one of my "lights" straight into his ribs. Someone else must have also seen him for at almost the same instant another arrow hit into him not six inches from mine.

We reaped a tremendous toll before the men on the Venetian's deck realised what was happening and began to seek cover by diving down behind its deck railing. But that did not stop the Venetian captain from running alongside of us or turning towards us. He is a brave man and there is no doubt about it—our paths are converging and we are about to rub the sides of our galleys together.

"Ship your oars; ship your oars," was the desperate shout from our sailing sergeant as the Venetian suddenly lurched over towards us and started to rub up against our port side.

The sides of the two galleys literally bounced off each other several times. As I stumbled against the railing, I could clearly hear the crack and screams as oars in both galleys were broken off and others were suddenly snapped back with bone-breaking force against their rowers' chests and faces.

When the galleys finish bouncing off each other and the distance between their hulls began to widen, I regained my balance—and as I did I found myself staring across the narrow space between us into the face of a heavily bearded middle-aged Venetian with wild eyes, a snarling mouth, and a sword in his hand. He looked to be about my age and he was staring straight at me from less than twenty paces away.

Our eyes met—and then I watched as if time was standing still as his eyes widened in shocked surprise when I put a shaft right into his chest before he could get his shield up. *'Sorry, old man,' is what came into my mind; at this distance, I would never miss such a big target as you.*

***** *Guy from Margate*

Chaos is the only way to describe what is going on down below on our rowing benches. I have been a sailing sergeant for years and never seen such a sight in all my days. The Captain and Bishop Thomas are using their bows and have left the galley to me and George down below me. He is the rowing sergeant.

I kept shouting orders down to George, but our rowing stopped when we collided with the Venetian and we could not start rowing again until George got the rowers organised and their oars back in the water. I would have gone down there myself to sort things out, but I am supposed to stay up here.

It seemed to take forever as I watched our oarsmen pass unbroken oars to each other and reseat themselves. Finally, George got the drum started and we began to pick up speed once again. Thank God the bastard who hit us is still dead in the water. *Oh sweet Jesus. Here comes another.*

"Hurry, George; hurry, goddamn it. Here comes another of the bastards."

***** *Thomas*

Our rowing stopped briefly after we sideswiped the Venetian and that was all it took for some of the Venetian galleys behind us to begin to catch us up. Three of them were coming up fast and were almost on us.

After our three closest pursuers, there appeared to be quite a gap—I could not make out any others due to all the hulls and masts in the harbour between them and us. Three's more than enough to catch us, however, particularly since some of our rowers may have been injured when their oars snapped back and many of our archers are on deck with their longbows.

"We are coming to the other entrance to the harbour," Jeffrey shouted as he pointed.

"Dead ahead." After a pause, he added, "Dear God, look."

My heart sank when I looked where Jeffrey was pointing. I could see past the hulls of the handful of transports anchored in this less-used part of the harbour and there was no doubt about it—the Venetians had some of their galleys waiting at this entrance as well. Worse, their rowers would be fresh and ours were not.

From somewhere in the back of my mind an idea emerged.

"Jeffrey," I shouted. "It is time for us to stop and reorganise, and then do what they do not expect. Do you still have the Venetian flags from the prizes we took?"

# Chapter Sixteen

*A desperate effort.*

Jeffrey listened to my idea, and gave me a tight smile and nod of acceptance. He immediately began giving the necessary orders. I watched anxiously as our men ran to change their positions and some of the wounded men sheltering in the stern castle came out to help. It was as if time was standing still.

Our galley slowed down rapidly, too rapidly, as our sailors and archers began changing positions. The three Venetians chasing after us began closing the distance between us and them.

The archers on the deck and in the lookout's nest have the freshest arms, so they hurried down to the lower rowing deck where the oars are lighter as well as being both more effective and easier to quickly bring inside our hull because they are shorter.

They were joined there by everyone who also had not rowed yet including the rowing sergeant, the drummer, Jeffrey's talking sergeant, and most of the sailors. The longer stroke oars on the last four benches on each side soon had two fresh rowers on them and so did the even bigger rudder oars.

After only a few frenzied seconds, every oar on the lower deck had at least one man with fresh arms on it. Then we rapidly swung around to go back the way we would just come—with three of our wounded men gamely waving

Venetian flags from positions on the deck and fresh archers from our rowing benches climbing the mast to the lookout's nest with their bows, all the quivers they could carry, and some of the Venetian flags we had taken from our prizes.

The sailors who had been carrying arrows up the mast were now rowing so one of the archers who had been rowing will carry additional arrows up to them as needed. He had stay on the deck and use his longbow when he was not carrying arrows to the lookout's nest.

The changeover to add fresh rowers went rather smoothly as well it should—thanks to my friend Harold, we require changing rowers and archers in a hurry be practised every day on every one of our galleys.

Our sail was going up, Venetian flags were being waved by some of our wounded men, and many of the exhausted rowers from the lower benches were resting on deck with their longbows as the rowing drum began to beat and we got underway once again. We would be moving even faster now as we go downwind with the wind filling the sail.

We were as ready as we could be. The archers now on the deck will be joined by the archers now resting on the upper tier of rowing benches if there is any close-quarters fighting on deck or more archers are needed.

*****

The closest of the trailing Venetian galleys was almost on top of us by the time I ran down the steps to the rowers on the lower bank of oars and Jeffrey spun us around so we can head back the way we came—and straight at our pursuers.

I saw the closest Venetian before I rushed down to the rowers.  It was a galley like ours with two banks of oars and so were the two galleys behind it.  The first of them would be on us almost instantly.

"Be ready to pull them in fast, boys."

That was what I shouted over and over again to the rowers as I ran down the narrow aisle between the lower rowing benches.  Our rowing drum was beating but not all that fast. Jeffrey was on the deck commanding the archers.

***** *Jeffrey*

Thomas was down on the first tier of benches getting the new rowers settled in, both my voice and my sailing sergeant were on the oars, and I was all by myself on the castle roof as we turned and almost immediately closed with the first of the pursuing Venetians.

The Venetian galley coming at us was rowing hard using both tiers of oars. He obviously wanted to disable us by breaking out our oars just as we want to do the same to him if we can break them without getting damaged or slowed in the process. At the moment, we were only rowing with our lower bank of oars for just that reason—because they are shorter and easier to pull in.

The first Venetian is almost on us. I can see the men on the Venetian's deck waving their swords and I can see our archers pouring arrows into them. *They do not even have archers with short bows, the fools.*

"Stand by to ship oars. Stand by. Ship oars. Ship oars."

Our men were primed and ready and our oars come in fast, very fast. Within seconds, there was a great grinding and lurching as our hulls scraped together with the unmistakable cracking and crunching noise as oars are broken and screams as those that do not break snap back at their oarsmen—hopefully, all theirs because I think all ours got shipped in time.

The Venetian grinding along our starboard side virtually stopped us dead in the water as it went past. And I could see one of the other Venetian thrusters going on by port side without getting close enough to take off any of her oars. Now, where the hell is the third one?

"Out lower bank oars. Out lower bank oars. Row easy, boys, row easy."

I never did see the third Venetian. And I did not have time to look for him—I was too busy watching the Venetians on the deck of the galley going past and shouting commands down to the rudder men and the rowers on the lower bank of oars as we began to go back through the mass of cogs and ships in the Venice harbour.

We were only rowing the lower oars, our sail was up, and we were waving Venetian flags and not rowing hard. Men were lining the decks of the boats we pass and some of the men even waved as we slowly slid past them.

Numerous Venetian galleys were pulling hard and coming the other way. Twice, we come close to galleys coming right at us—and rowed slowly and serenely right on past them because they did not realise we were not one of theirs until it was too late. The arrows of our archers swept their decks as we went past.

Thomas joined me on the roof of the castle and ten minutes later we passed out of the harbour entrance and into the sea ahead. The sea was clear ahead of us all the way to the horizon but we were not out of the woods yet—looking back, I could see that we have a number of pursuers. They had turned around to follow us and we are hours away from the sun finishing its pass over the earth so it would be dark enough for us to slip away. We have got our sail up and so do all of them.

"How many are still behind us do you think?" I asked Thomas.

***** *Thomas*

Our rowing drum began to pick up the beat and the fresh arms of the archers on our upper tier of oars finally began to row as the first of our pursuers closed on us. The other two Venetians, and at least two more according to the lookouts on our mast, were coming up behind us as well. Jeffrey himself scampered up the mast for a look.

"There are at least four more galleys behind the first two and they are all coming hard using all their oars and their sails," he shouted to me breathlessly as he began to climb back down.

Our rowing drum picked up the pace, and Jeffrey sent everyone on the deck back to the oars. We now have two men on every oar on the lower tier and one man on every oar on the top tier stroking at every other drum beat.

An hour passed and another started. We held our speed and our flight went on. Exhausted rowers were relieved and took over the carrying of the water skins and bread from rower to rower until it was their turn to row again.

Our pursuers all stayed with us. They must have added their fighting men and sailors to the slaves who normally do their rowing.

Several times one or another of our pursuers tried to put on a burst of speed and catch us. Neither succeeded in accomplishing anything except exhausting its rowers before it began falling back.

***** *Sergeant Captain Jeffrey*

The wind was from the west when I came down from yet another look from the mast and slowly reduced the rowing beat. Almost an hour or so earlier, one of the Venetians who had been further back was able catch up and pass the two galleys which had previously been in front.

The thruster and one other were now the only Venetians in sight—and they both followed us and cut the corner to close rapidly when I suddenly made a dogleg turn to the left. Hopefully, we and our two closest pursuers were far enough ahead of the other Venetian galleys so their lookouts did not see any of us make the turn. *I pray to God they did not see our two closest pursuers make the turn and follow us.*

"Andrew," I shouted to one of my sailors who had recently been replaced on the upper tier so he can take his turn going for water and taking a piss. "Climb the mast all the way to the top and keep a lookout. Take another quiver of arrows up to the nest, but climb on past it and go as high as you can go. Leave everything else here on the deck with me. You will need both hands to hold on tight."

*Andrew's got good eyes; he will see them if anyone will.*

Twenty minutes later and it is almost certain only two of our pursuers made the turn to follow us. The Venetians further back missed our turn and are no longer a threat. We are sailing and rowing with the wind in our sail coming from our port side.

Now it is just between us and our two remaining pursuers. Well, it is just between us and them if Andrew's right about none of the other Venetians making the turn to follow us. In any event, the closest of our two pursuers was finally closing on us.

I stopped the top tier of oars from rowing and ordered the archers from the top tier to come on deck as our nearest pursuer continued to close the gap between us. I let the Venetian close on us until it was well within the range of our archers. Then I gave the word and our archers began to launch.

****** *Thomas*

I myself climbed part way up the mast to watch as the archers on our deck began to push out their arrows.

*I have only tried to climb a mast a few times before and it is not something I enjoy. The damn ropes are often wet and slippery, and the mast sways back and forth and it sometimes gives a sudden jerk when we hit a bigger than usual wave.*

In the distance I could see movement on the deck of our closest pursuer as the arrows of our archers found the range and a steady stream of arrows began to drop on to the deck of the closest Venetian. The tables were turning. At first, the Venetian thruster merely slowed down to drop back out of range. But we slowed with it so it could not escape the continuous and expertly aimed rain of our archers' arrows.

Finally, the Venetian had had enough and turned to break off. We kept going and our lookouts were soon reporting only one Venetian galley in sight behind us. It was early in the afternoon.

***** *Thomas*

For more than an hour Jeffrey tantalised the pursuing Venetian by staying just far enough ahead of him to avoid contact, as we led him further and further away from where we thought the other Venetian galleys might be searching. What Jeffrey was doing is something that has worked for us over and over again in the past with the Moors—the "wounded bird" manoeuver Harold teaches all our captains.

"What do you think?" Jeffrey asked me after the lookout on our mast responded to his hailed inquiry by once again reporting only a few fishing boats are in sight in addition to the galley chasing after us.

"It is time," I agreed with a nod.

Jeffrey turned to let the wind fill our sail and once again our rowing drum slowed to allow our Venetian pursuer to come closer. When it was close enough, our archers began sending a storm of arrows into it—and this one surprised us by shooting back with crossbow quarrels.

To our amazement, one of our archers went down with a crossbow quarrel in his forehead. It killed him instantly and caused the arrow he was about to launch to go skittering off into the sea—and that caused his cursing, fellow archers to redouble their efforts to drop their arrows on to the men on our pursuer's deck and its rudder men.

Finally, the Venetians had enough and turned to break off contact—and this time we turned back to go after them.

Jeffrey quickly spun our galley around using both its rudder and oars and then we rowed hard with both banks of oars until we reached a position slightly behind and slightly off to the port side of our now fleeing prey. From this angle the arrows of our archers could drop into the open area behind the Venetian's mast and reach down to its rudder men and some of its rowers—and they mostly did.

Within minutes, the Venetian was virtually stopped with its deck and its upper tier of rowing benches clear of men.

The Venetian captain, however, was not a fool. At some point he realised our need to have a specific position if our archers are to drop arrows into the open area next to his lower rowing benches where his rudder men stand.

He responded wisely—by having his rowers in his lower tier of oars periodically rowing on only one side so that his galley keeps turning in a tight circle to keep us from having clear shots.

It was almost a game. The Venetian captain was constantly using the oars in his lower tier to swing his galley around so as to deny our archers a shooting line into his rudder men and the open area on his lower deck where his survivors are hiding—and Jeffrey was constantly manoeuvring his galley around the Venetian's galley so our archers could drop arrows on to them. And it was not all one-sided—twice one of our archers was hit with a crossbow quarrel, one of them with a wound almost certain to be fatal.

Jeffrey finally brought us alongside the Venetian just before the sun began to go down. The archers on our deck and in the lookout's nest had already cleared the Venetian's deck and the upper rowing benches of everyone they could see before Jeffrey brought us in alongside the Venetian.

The Venetian's deck was empty as our sailors threw their grappling irons to grab its deck railing, lines, and anything else their hooks can catch. With the sun almost finished passing overhead, it was now or never if we are going to make the Venetians pay for the trouble they have caused us.

The shuddering crash as the two hulls came together brought the surviving Venetians desperately charging out to repel boarders from behind the nearside deck railing where they had been sheltering from our archers.

Other screaming and shouting Venetians come charging up out of the Venetian's lower rowing deck—and they all ran straight into an absolute storm of arrows delivered at close range by the archers lining the side of our galley.

For an instant Jeffrey and I and every archer on the deck were shooting arrows at close range as the Venetians launched their forlorn hope and went down with screams and cries. The handful of survivors quickly dropped back down behind the Venetian's deck railing to cower and try to stay out of sight.

For a few minutes, the two galleys bobbed up and down together on the waves and there was no movement on the Venetian. All we could see are a couple of bodies on the Venetian's deck.

It was somewhat of a standoff because neither captain dared to send a man up his galley's mast as a lookout for fear he will be picked off by an archer. Even so, for almost an hour we made no attempt to board. We had won; there was no sense risking the loss of more men by starting a needless fight.

Finally, there was a loud hail in Italian, "Quarter. Quarter. We surrender."

That was when Jeffrey surprised me by saying something he probably picked up from one of Harold's training sessions for the men who are the sergeant captains of our galleys and cogs.

*If Harold did not say it, he should.*

"Hunters do not do well when they become the hunted, do they? It is something they do not expect until it is too late."

***** *Thomas*

A goodly number of the Venetian crew's sailors and soldiers were dead or wounded, almost all of them. So were many of their galley slaves. They got hit by the arrows our archers were dropping into the lower rowing benches in an effort to get the Venetian's rudder men. The poor sods were chained in place and could not get to cover.

"I know how you feel about the slaves, but what should we do with the Venetians," Jeffrey asked me, "drop the bastards over the side? Tried to kill us, did not they?"

My response was rather sharp and it caused a look of concern to pass over Jeffrey's face.

"It is not how I feel about the slaves, Jeffrey. It is what William ordered be done if any slaves are taken—you are to free them as soon as possible. He really meant it, Jeffrey; you will be lucky to lose only your stripes and command if ever you do not obey his orders about the treatment of serfs and slaves."

*But I really am torn about the Venetians. Maybe we should just throw them overboard the way we did with the five crews that tried to pirate us. They did, after all, try to attack us.*

Finally, I decided.

"Free the wounded slaves and put the Venetians in their chains, even the wounded ones. We will free the rest of the slaves when we have more men. The Venetians who are able can help row until we can send them off to the Holy Land." *Or maybe we can exchange them for a ransom or some Englishmen if they are holding any. Hmm, that is an idea; yes, it is.*

"Come on, Jeffrey, let's go see if any of their slaves are British or French."

Darkness was falling as our rowing drum began its beat and we started our long voyage back to England—but it would not be direct, I decided. So I returned to the little castle in the bow and began rummaging through my things to find a blank parchment and a goose feather and the little pouch of charcoal I use to make ink.

# Chapter Seventeen

*Our generous offer.*

The early light before dawn the next morning found us once again approaching the entrance to Venice's harbour. A small prize crew was taking the Venetian galley to Cyprus. It was sailing with most of the Venetians chained to the rowing benches except for three badly wounded men who may or may not survive. The slaves will be freed when they reach Cyprus; so will the Venetians, although they do not know it yet. The only Venetian not sailing for Cyprus is the wounded captain. He is with us.

Jeffrey was more than a little nervous about my plan and said as much.

"I do not like this, Thomas. What if they are waiting for us?"

"Nonsense. No one knows we are coming back for Cardinal Bertoli. It is the last thing they would expect us to do."

*****

We passed through the harbour entrance just as the sun peeped over the horizon. We rowed straight to the same quay where we had been moored yesterday. No one paid us any attention at all as we went past the transports anchored in the harbour with the oars of our lower rowing deck swishing and a Venetian flag flying.

"Do you understand, Captain? This is for the Doge." I asked the Venetian galley captain in French and in Latin as we approached the quay and I handed him the parchment I had spent several hours scribing by the light of a galley lantern.

*I think he understands. Well, I guess we will know soon enough.*

"Si, Signore, al Doge; al Doge."

A minute or so later we bumped up against the quay. Jeffrey's sailors used their pikes to hold us in place whilst several of them climbed up to the quay so they could help pull the wounded captain up from our galley. He winced as they pulled and we pushed on his arse, but he made it.

As soon as the captain reached the quay, Jeffrey's sailors jumped back down on to the deck and we began moving away to wait several hours south of the harbour entrance.

*****

The men rested and ate to restore their strength whilst we waited. We waited all day long and into the night as a steady stream of cogs and other transports came and went from the busy harbour.

We moved back towards the harbour entrance and were on high alert as dawn approached. If an effort was to be made to take us, it would be now. There were four archers in the lookout's nest and a sailor with good eyes further up above them at the very top of the mast.

"Sail, Hoy," shouted lookouts several times as transports began coming out as soon as there was enough light. Then it came, "Sail, Hoy. There is a galley coming out. It is rowing with its lower oars and its deck is clear; no lookouts on the mast."

The Venetian galley had no lookouts on its mast so we saw it before it saw us. We waited with our oars fully manned and ready to run—and our best archers on deck ready to launch if it is a ruse.

*So far, so good.*

I myself immediately climbed part way up the mast so I could see its deck. And there he was all alone on the roof of the Venetian's bow castle—Cardinal Bertoli. The only other man in sight was a Venetian on the roof of the stern castle as I had specified in my parchment. As the gap between galleys closed, I could see a big smile on Bertoli's face as he came off the castle roof and walked to the deck railing.

The Venetian shipped its oars and wallowed in the waves as we approached. Jeffrey was taking no chances as we came alongside. He had men with pikes to hold our hulls together and men with swords ready to cut any grapples that might be thrown. None were.

Two of Jeffrey's biggest and strongest sailors followed me to our railing and then, as they obviously had done many times before, they leaned across the railing and each took a firm hold of one of the Cardinal's arms and swung him aboard. "Push off," an anxious Jeffrey shouted to his pike men as I gave Bertoli a big, welcoming hug.

"I thought I was dreaming when they came and told me I was to be freed. I thought they were coming to kill me. How did you do it?"

"I made the Venetians an offer they could not refuse," I explained. "I told them we would either be sailing this morning for Rome with you or we would begin taking or burning all the

Venetian galleys and cogs we could find starting with all those in the harbour—and they could choose."


- End of the Book –

# There are more books in *The Company of Archers Saga*.

All of the books in this exciting and action-packed medieval saga are available on Amazon as individual eBooks. Some of them are also available in print and as audio books. Many of them are available in multi-book collections. You can find them by searching for *Martin Archer Stories*.

There is a bargain-priced collection containing all of first six books of the saga. A similar collection of the next four books in the saga is available as *The Archers' Story: Part II;* the three novels after that are collected as *The Archers' Story Part III;* and the four after that as *The Archers' Story: Part IV.* There is also a *Part V* with the next three.

A chronological list of all the books in the saga, and other books by Martin Archer, can be found below along with a few sample pages from the first book in the saga.

Finally, a word from Martin:

"I sincerely hope you enjoyed reading the stories about the hard men of Britain's first great merchant company as much as I have enjoyed writing it. If so, I hope you will consider reading the other stories in the saga and leaving a favourable review on Amazon or Google with as many stars as possible in order to encourage other readers.

"And, if you could please spare a moment, I would also very much appreciate your thoughts and suggestions about this saga and its stories. Should the stories continue? What do you think? I can be reached at martinarcherV@gmail.com."

Cheers and thank you once again. /S/ Martin Archer

**Books in the exciting and action-packed *The Company of Archers* saga:**

*The Archers*

*The Archers' Castle*

*The Archers' Return*

*The Archers' War*

*Rescuing the Hostages*

*Archers and Crusaders*

*The Archers' Gold*

*The Missing Treasure*

*Castling the King*

*The Sea Warriors*

*The Captain's Men*

*Gulling the Kings*

*The Magna Carta Decision*

*The War of the Kings*

*The Company's Revenge*

*The Ransom*

*The New Commander*

*The Gold Coins*

*The Emperor has no Gold*

*Protecting the Gold:  The Fatal Mistakes*

*The Alchemist's Revenge*

*The Venetian Gambit*

*Today's Friends*

*The English Gambits*


**eBooks in Martin Archer's epic *Soldiers and Marines* saga:**

*Soldiers and Marines*

*Peace and Conflict*

*War Breaks Out*

*War in the East  (A fictional tale of America's role in the next great war)*

*Israel's Next War (A prescient book much hated by Islamic reviewers)*

**Collections of Martin Archer's books on Amazon**

*The Archers Stories I* - complete books I, II, III, IV, V, and VI

*The Archers Stories II* - complete books VII, VIII, IX, and X

*The Archers Stories III* - complete books XI, XII, and XIII

*The Archers Stories IV* – complete books XIV, XV, XVI, and XVII

*The Archers Stories V* – complete books XVIII, XIX, and XX

*The Soldiers and Marines Saga* - complete books I, II, and III

**Other eBooks you might enjoy:**

*Cage's Crew* by Martin Archer writing as Raymond Casey

*America's Next War* by Michael Cameron – an adaption of Martin Archer's *War Breaks Out* to set it in the immediate future when Eastern and Western Europe go to war over another wave of Islamic refugees.

Made in the USA
Las Vegas, NV
01 January 2024